SHADOWS OF A TIME PAST

SHADOWS OF A TIME PAST

PAST

- The Demons of Chucaya -

Dominic Perenzin

iUniverse, Inc.

New York Lincoln Shanghai

SHADOWS OF A TIME PAST
- The Demons of Chucaya -

iUniverse books may be ordered through booksellers or by contacting:

iUniverse
2021 Pine Lake Road, Suite 100
Lincoln, NE 68512
www.iuniverse.com
1-800-Authors (1-800-288-4677)

ISBN: 0-595-34563-8

Printed in the United States of America

Be It Known To The Public

That, on the sunless morning of August 18, 1634, in the Village of Loudun, France, there was a palpable foreboding in the air as a multitude of people stood silently outside the courthouse. Inside, all the benches were occupied by the gentry not only of Loudun itself but also from the surrounding towns. Wives and daughters were richly attired in the finest satin and velvet gowns and bejeweled in precious stones. All waited anxiously for the final judgment of a special panel of judges.

A door of the courtroom opened wide and standing there the solitary figure of the accused, the Jesuit-educated parish priest of St. Pierre du Marché, Father Urbain Grandier, dressed in his nightgown and slippers.

Two priests in full ceremonial vestments entered, and with rehearsed solemnity proceeded to sprinkle holy water on everything in sight.

Hands tied behind his back, the accused was led across the room and made to kneel before the judges' bench.

The clerk of the court stepped forward, adjusted his reading glasses, cleared his throat and looked around the room to assure himself that he had everyone's attention. When assured of this, he began to read.

Father Urbain Grandier was accused of sorcery, magic, maleficia and causing the demoniacal possession of several Ursuline nuns as well as of other secular women, compelling them to fall into a state of absolute depravity.

After reading several pages of standard legalese, during which fidgeting and murmurs of impatience could be heard throughout the courtroom the clerk arrived at the court's decision; he paused for a moment, then in a cold official tone announced:

Guilty As Accused

A collective release of breath could be heard followed again by silence as the clerk announced the sentence:

Death At The Stake
-To be proceeded by Ordinary and Extraordinary Tortures-

A wave of sighs swept across the courtroom, two women fainted.

Pursuant to the pre-established rules fixed specifically for this special proceeding, Grandier was allowed to address the judges.

"My Lords, I call God the Father, God the Son and God the Holy Ghost to witness, together with the Virgin my sole advocate, that I have never committed sacrilege and have never known any magic other than the Holy Scripture, for which I have always preached. I adore my Savior and pray that I may partake in the merit of the blood of his passion."

He looked up into the faces of the judges and his heart became heavy as he saw they were unmoved by his words.

The condemned priest was taken to a solitary place where, after having his nightgown removed, was bound and stretched out on the floor. Next to him was the dreaded box of torture, the infamous Boot, a wooden square made up of four parallel oaken boards, two outer pairs fixed and unmovable, and two movable inner pairs.

From his knees to his feet the priest's legs were placed between the inner and outer boards. In the space between the two inner boards wooden wedges of progressively larger sizes could be driven in, pushing the inner boards outwards and squeezing the legs ever tighter.

As each wedge was driven down with the macabre thud of the huge mallet, Grandier screamed in pain and called upon the Lord.

The priest Father Lactance ordered him to confess. Grandier responded, "Father, do you believe in your conscience that a man to be delivered from pain, must confess to a crime he had not committed?"

Father Lantance, interpreting this as deceptive talk and sophistry of the Devil, continued to insist on an admission of guilt. More wedges were driven into the Boot, more bones cracked and more blood flowed.

Grandier said he would confess that being a man he had known women. Unsatisfied, Lactance said no, that was not enough, he must admit to sorcery. Grandier replied that he could not do so and called upon God as his witness. The priest said what Grandier was really doing was calling upon the Devil and not God, and ordered the tenth wedge be driven in.

Grandier appeared to be on the verge of passing out. Lactance was near panic, this must not be allowed to happen, he must be awake and conscious for the stake, for his suffering must be the greatest possible. He was removed from the Boot and placed on the stone slab in a cold damp cell where light was uninvited.

More than six thousand persons crammed into the public square of St. Croix, some stood on surrounding rooftops and on the gargoyles of the church. Every window not used by the owner had been rented out. A grandstand was put up in the square for the judges and Grandier's enemies.

Near the wall of the church a solid, thick fifteen-foot pole had been driven into the ground, above its base logs and straw were piled up in layers and maggots were strewn about. Because Grandier's crushed legs would make it impossible for him to stand, an iron chair was fastened to the pole a few short feet above the firewood.

All was now ready for the company of archers who entered the square followed by six mules drawing a cart in which Father Urbain Grandier sat. Arriving at the post, he was taken down from the cart, placed on the iron seat and securely fastened to the post.

He felt the touch of a hand on his shoulder, it was La Grange, the Captain of the Guard. He wanted Grandier's forgiveness for what he was obligated to do, and made two promises: Grandier would be allowed to speak, and he would be strangled before the fire was ignited.

Holy water was sprinkled over the wood, the straw, the condemned, the executioners, the earth, the air, the spectators, even the glowing coals of the brazier. Grandier was to suffer to the maximum and no chance would be taken that the Devil should appear to prevent this from happening.

When Grandier tried to speak, holy water was thrown in his face.

"Confess your sin, you have only a moment left to live," shouted Father Lactance.

"Only a moment and I must go to that just and fearful judgment to which, Reverend Father, you too must soon be called."

Angered, Father Lactance cast his torch on the straw of the pyre. The flames began to spread.

Sympathetic cries of "strangle him, strangle, strangle," came from the crowd.

La Grange ordered the executioner to place the noose around Grandier's neck, but someone had surreptitiously knotted the rope, rendering it impossible to use.

More torches were thrown on the pyre.

From beyond the wall of flames came screams and cries of anguish so intense that they rent the hearts of many in the crowd, then a convulsion of coughing. Believing perhaps that Grandier with the help of the Devil was attempting to cheat them by dying of suffocation, Father Lactance threw holy water on the smoke and flames.

Hours later, when finally the embers of fire had died out and the darkness of the late afternoon had spread across the square, a few spectators converged on the blackened remains and, burning their fingers in the process, poked around the dust hunting for the charred remains of teeth, fragments of the skull and ribs to be used as amulets against future evils.

CHAPTER 1

▼

On this sunny morning of March 14, 2002 in the city of Atlanta in the State of Georgia, Ted Shaw got out of his car, looked across the street and there it was staring him in the face, "Claremount Elementary School" spread over the arched entrance to the building. Another responsibility he was about to assume with the death of his wife. A reminder of the number of things she routinely attended to of which he had perfunctory knowledge but had failed to appreciate. Guess I was too immersed in my own world of professional concerns, he thought.

The staccato horn of a school bus jerked him out of his momentary reverie, the driver motioning him to close his car door to let the bus pass without incident. He apologetically closed the door and unnecessarily pressed his body against the car as the bus passed. Looking inside the car he spotted the note on the passenger's seat, went around to the other side, opened the door and picked it up. "Alice Reddy, Room 211, 10:15 a.m. March 14."

As he crossed the street, he noticed that on the side of the school building broad, fading letters informed the public that four years earlier the school had received an award for "Excellence in Education." Wonder what's been happening since then, he thought, sounds like it's been down hill since then. Yet, he knew the school had a good reputation. Mentally shrugging his shoulders he entered the building.

Walking down the corridor looking for Room 211, Ted Shaw for the second time this day questioned the importance of a parent-teacher meeting to discuss a five-year-old kindergartener's progress, or lack of it. From what he had seen, about all these kids seem to do is to make drawings, sketches and that kind of stuff.

Arriving at Room 211, he knocked lightly and opened the door a crack when a voice from within asked that he please wait a few moments. He closed the door and with hands in pockets leaned against the wall. Along the corridor there were a number of whom he presumed were other parents waiting to enter classrooms. But he was the only male. Guess the fathers are where I should be, he thought. But he no longer had a wife to fall back on for this chore. His sister-in-law Lucille would have filled in for him had he asked but somehow it didn't seem right to Cindy. Moreover, Lucille had already been indispensably helpful since her sister's death.

Oh well, he resigned himself to the fact he was about to lose a total of an hour or so on an event devoid of any real importance in his life. How many such lost hours had he accumulated during his lifetime, hours lost in the Black Hole of wasted time. Perhaps he should have brought his laptop with him, but again, he would have had to sit on the floor to use it, and he was not about to do that.

For the second time in the last half hour an internal monologue was interrupted, this time by the opening of the Room 211 door as a woman carrying a handful of papers containing sketches and numbers stepped out with a smile of self-satisfaction on her plump face. Looks like her little girl is doing all right, thought Ted.

"I'm Cindy Shaw's father," he said by way of introduction as he extended his hand.

"Nice to meet you Mr. Shaw and thanks for coming. I'm Miss Reddy" she said as she shook the extended hand. "Please have a seat."

As she gathered papers together from a folder marked Cindy Shaw, Ted, with what he realized was a silly grin on his, studied her face. How young, he thought, probably freshly minted by some college's education department. He didn't recall his teachers ever being that young.

Ms. Reddy commenced explaining how well Cindy had done over the last grading period, while Ted noticed the lovely manner her lips shaped words. Realizing what was occurring the teacher shifted in her chair. It was not until she placed one of Cindy's drawings in front of him that his attention was fully drawn to the meaning of her words.

"As you can see, Cindy shows signs of talent. Notice the variety of scenes, good imagination, don't you agree?" Ted tilted his head to one side and nodded in agreement. He saw how slender and lovely shaped her hands were as they turned the papers. "Curious isn't it that she would color all of the people blue, look here." Before what he was looking at registered in his distracted attention, he had uttered, "Yes, strange isn't it."

After a slight pause, he wrinkled his brow as if trying to recall an illusive thought then explained that he believed there really might be blue-skin people in the world. The teacher gave him a questioning look causing him to add that at least that was what he was told way back in college by a foreign student from Zambilla. Unless his memory failed him, there was a tribe of Indians living in the mountainous central part of that country, sierras he thought they were called, who had blue skin. However, he was sure he never mentioned this to Cindy.

"How fascinating," commented the teacher. Her major at Fordham was anthropology and she didn't recall ever hearing or reading about such a tribe, which she guessed didn't necessarily mean they didn't exist. She took back the sketch and placed it in a folder with the rest of Cindy's work-product which she then handed to the father. A few final comments on how well the student was doing and the meeting was over.

While waiting for the next parent, two thoughts played in Ms. Reddy's mind: blue skinned people and how handsome and suave Cindy's father was.

On his way to his office the surface of Ted's consciousness was on business matters that awaited his attention, but in the deeper recesses something had been touched that kept elbowing his office thoughts.

*   *   *   *

October 11, 1995 in the office of the abbess of the Saint Agnes Convent outside of the South American town of Chucaya, Zambilla, Sister Dolores des Anges sat behind her plain metal desk; in front of her sat two priests, one in his mid-thirties and the second in his late-seventies.

The first to speak was the elderly priest.

"Sister, I want you to meet Father Manfredo who has recently arrived here from the Sacred Heart Church in Santa Fe. As you know, I have made a decision to retire these weary bones and will be returning to Italy where, on a much-reduced level, I intend to place what energy remains to the service of the Church and the Holy Father. Father Manfredo is my replacement."

"Yes, I am aware of your decision and must say you will be dearly missed by all of us, but if God had ordained that this should be then we must take solace in His infinite wisdom."

This she said with head held high, eyes fixed on the top of her desk like someone who, though convinced of her self-importance and exalted rank, finds it necessary to accede to distasteful mandates from an even higher hierarchical source.

"I am confident that to whatever activities lie ahead, you will bring the wealth of your years of experience and devotion to the service of God," she added, raising her eyes towards the old priest with the faint hint of a smile.

"You are too kind to this humble servant of God," answered the old priest, "but I am confident that Father Manfredo will carry on with even greater merit the work of Our Lord here in this beautiful and holy place. Father Manfredo..."

Interrupting, the young priest raised both hands, palms facing out as if warding something off and with conviction said, "It would truly be a miracle if someone could replace you Father Roberto, the best I can do is to try to emulate what you have done."

Continuing on, the elderly priest said that Father Manfredo had been fully informed of the practices and schedule he had been following in the Convent, such as masses, confessions, etc...This did not mean changes could not be made, that would be up to the abbess and Father Manfredo to work out.

After a few more minutes of pleasantries, the two priests were about to exit the room when the abbess asked the elder priest if he could remain for a moment. The two priests agreed to meet later in front of the chapel. The young priest closed the door behind him.

"Father Roberto" began the nun, "you will forgive me if I appear ungrateful, overly concerned or unjustifiably anticipating certain inconveniences, but as you are aware, for the most part our sisters are young and yes, they are devoted to their vocation in the service of Our Lord, nevertheless, they are young and impressionable. As you know, it is a firm rule of the Convent that men are not permitted to pass beyond its walls, the sole exception being the priest who celebrates mass and hears confessions here, as in your case. Even the doctors who come here are women. The point I am trying to make is that your replacement seems so young, enough so as to perhaps become a distraction. Frankly, I am concerned. Would it not be possible, and the Lord forgive me for giving the impression that I lack respect for Father Manfredo or question for a moment his true devotion, that Father Alias from your St. Anthony Church could carry on for you, after all he has been here and knows the Convent and the sisters know him."

There was a moment of silence as the elderly priest slowly nodded his head in a gesture of sympathetic understanding.

"Sister, I admire the depth of your concern over your flock. The selection of Father Manfredo was made by the Bishop and, as you are aware, this may not be modified by anyone but him. Father Alias, God bless him, carries upon his shoulders only a few years less than I. His health has greatly deteriorated, so much so that he is now obliged to spend much time resting each day. But do not be concerned, Father Manfredo is very devoted to his calling and is wise far beyond his years."

Sister Dolores offered an uncomfortable smile of resignation.

The Convent's prioress provided the young priest with a tour of the important areas of the Convent grounds. She was short in height but long in conversation. She explained that the Convent had been designed to be a close replica of the type of monastery idealized by Saint Benedict of Nursia back around the year 529.

Walking along a path next to the stonewall that encircled the cloister, the sister explained that the walls had initially been built as a defense against the unfriendly natives, and that today they functioned as a border separating the secular external world from the spiritual world of the cloister.

A centrally located space within the enclosure contained a grass courtyard with stone-paved paths leading to a fountain in the center, like spokes of a wheel to a hub. The single entrance to the Convent was through an enormously thick 12-foot wooden door built originally large enough to allow horse-drawn carriages to pass. In its center, a smaller door through which people could enter and leave. The priest wondered but did not ask how the nuns were able to move such a large door.

On the eastern side of the grounds were a series of upper-level meditation rooms beneath which was the single dormitory. Benedictine custom going back centuries was for communal steeping quarters rather than individual cells as in other convents. The meditation rooms were connected to the church by a day stair leading down to an arcaded passageway, past the dormitory to the entrance to the church. Next to the church was a small building in which on Saturdays the nuns provided religious classes for young girls up to the age of 12.

A single dining room together with an adjoining kitchen served the nun's basic secular need. Work places where the sisters performed their daily labors of knitting and sewing, shoe repairing, carpentry, carving wooden religious figures were located down the corridor.

"All work in the cloister is done by the nuns following Saint Benedict's dictum that idleness is the enemy of the soul," explained the prioress.

On the west side, three blocks had been removed from the stone wall and the opening fitted with latched doors through which supplies and donations were received, across from which there were two rooms, one for storage and the other for clerical work. All of the Convent's paper work was done in longhand.

Above these rooms was an infirmary with four beds, a room for examinations and a single medical supplies pantry. Most of the services were performed here by two nuns who had received rudimentary nurse training. Doctors were allowed into the Convent only for extremely urgent cases, but, as the prioress emphasized, only women doctors.

The north side of the grounds was devoted to gardening fruits, vegetables and flowers. The prioress pointed out how essential to the overall environment were the gardens for they were daily reminders of the natural beauty of God's creation. So important was this to the spiritual life of the sisters that each was assigned to work in the gardens for two or more weeks during the year.

Throughout the tour, which was conducted strictly from the outside of the various buildings, not a single nun was seen nor any sound heard. Father Manfredo was told the nuns were either in the meditation rooms or in the chapel reciting prayers, something they did several times a day. Outside the chapel's entrance the prioress and Father Manfredo found the elderly priest waiting. Imparting blessings on the prioress, the two priests left for Chucaya.

*   *   *   *

Ted had just dropped his daughter Cindy off at the school and was pulling away from the curb when his car was sideswiped. He got out to inspect the damage, but not before belittling the other driver as a stupid blind bastard. There were no apparent dents but some deep scratches along the door and fender. The driver of the other car remained seated in her vehicle, her head resting on the steering wheel. Having waited a few moments for her to make an appearance, Ted tapped on her window. The woman turned towards him, and they both widened their eyes in surprise. It was Alice Reddy, the teacher.

Hearing the sound of metal screeching against metal one of the school security personnel rushed to the scene and offered to call the police. Both drivers asked that he not do so since they could work this situation out on their own.

"Look," said the teacher turning to Ted Shaw, "I'm so sorry about this, I just didn't see you pulling out, are you alright?"

"I'm fine, I should've looked before pulling out."

"Please get an estimate of the damage to your car and I'll take care of it, I've got to get to my class, here's my telephone number."

"But it wasn't…" Ted started to say as the teacher drove off and into the faculty parking lot.

Later that afternoon as Alice Reddy entered her apartment the phone was ringing. "Hello, this is Ted Shaw, I'm calling about our accident today, I have the information we need to put this matter to bed."

"Really?" exclaimed Ms. Reddy, "you get fast results don't you."

"Tell you what, may I suggest we discuss this over dinner tonight, is your car alright?"

"Oh yes, it's running okay but it does have scratches from bumper to bumper which don't exactly add to its aesthetic qualities. As to dinner, I appreciate your invitation but I'm expecting company this evening."

"Well, let's make it tomorrow evening then."

"Can't you just tell me what the monetary damage is and hopefully I'll be able to take care of it out of my next paycheck?"

"There is something I must show you concerning the accident and the damage which is important." There was a brief interlude of silence except for the sound of background music coming from Ted's side. He continued, "We might as well add a touch of pleasantness to this unfortunate incident, don't you agree?"

The teacher was caught off-balance by this unexpected invitation, she had seen him once on what was a business-like parent-teacher meeting. While these thoughts bounced around her head, she heard her voice say okay, as if obedient to some autonomous part of her cerebral sphere.

"Fine, how about if I pick you up at eight."

"That will be alright, my address is…"

"Oh," he interrupted "I know your address, I'll see you tomorrow at eight, good night."

She held the phone to her ear until she heard the click from his end but not before she heard a few more strains of the music from his side, a blues tune and a girl singer she had heard before but couldn't name.

Later that evening as she was grading test papers, a part of her brain kept pulling her attention to the dinner invitation and about wanting to show her something. Could it be an estimate on the cost of repairing his car? If so, then it's probably written proof of the damage. I never did get out of my car to check his, so it could have been extensive. But why dinner? Some ulterior motive? Is he trying to hit on me, after all he did say something about putting the matter to bed.

Then she remembered, Oh shit, why did I say I'd try to pay out of my next paycheck? Sounds like I'm asking for some compassion. How embarrassing.

Later that night in bed and trying to get to the last page of a book she was reading, her mind again turned to the telephone call. The melody of the background music she heard kept playing in her mind when suddenly she sat up with a jerk saying, *You Call It Madness.* That was what she was singing and the singer is Diana Krall. How could I have not recognized her. I've got the CD I'm sure." She got out of bed to look for it. So he likes Diana Krall she thought, good taste. Maybe he found out I liked her, and he…well maybe not, but it's quite a coincidence she thought as she turned off the bedside lamp.

"Good evening Mr. Shaw" smiled the Maitre d' of the La Provence restaurant as he led the couple to their table. The teacher was impressed by the authenticity of the refined Old World décor, not that she had ever actually seen it in person, only in movies and books. Walking through the dining room, she noticed that the diners resembled those who appear in soap operas, so sophisticated and successful looking. Mr. Shaw must be someone of importance judging from the deference paid to him by the Maitre d'. Again, the illusiveness of why she had been invited here to talk about a car accident. She smiled at Ted Shaw who was standing across the table from her as the Maitre d' pulled her chair out for her.

At Ted's suggestion talk about the accident was postponed until after they had eaten. In the meantime, small talk flowed increasingly relaxed as the bottle of wine began losing its contents.

He was an executive of a national insurance company; birthplace, Bangor, Maine; Boston College undergrad and a Columbia University MBA; widower, his wife had died of cancer. Cindy was his only child.

The teacher was born in Barcelona, Spain, daughter of American parents, her father was an Air Force Colonel stationed in Spain. She had an undergraduate degree in anthropology from Fordham and was presently working as a substitute teacher while searching half-heartedly for employment more in line with her college major, though frankly she had reservations about a career in anthropology. She wasn't even sure why she ended up with that as her major.

Throughout dinner Ted Shaw proved to be an excellent conversationalist, knowledgeable in a pop-culture sort of way about a surprising range of topics which he brought up in the hope of finding one that interested her, weaving together questions about her with comments on himself, picking up on topics mentioned by her and turning them into subjects in which he seemed interested.

She estimated his age as between 40-45, a person clearly attentive to his physical appearance, trim of figure—probably went to a gym regularly—healthy, tight skin, smartly controlled energy and eyes that showed sincere interest in whatever she said.

Ted was attracted by her lovely face, a face that faintly reminded him of someone else, though he couldn't remember who it was. Her eyes clearly dominated her attractiveness, soft, at the same time lively and searching. But what fascinated him mostly about her physical features was the profile of her face. He was thoroughly enjoying her company and instantly decided he wanted to see more of her.

Both were relieved and pleased at how smoothly and increasingly relaxed their conversation had become. But as sherry was being poured she remembered the reason for the invitation and edged the conversation to the subject of the accident.

"I do want you to know how sorry I am about the accident. We should talk about it. I was late that morning and my mind was not exactly where it should have been. When I realized you were pulling out, now I don't remember whether I reached for the brakes and my foot slipped off and landed on the gas pedal or whether in momentary panic I stupidly stepped on the gas pedal. You know the rest of the story. Do you have an estimate of the costs of repairing your car?"

Not taking his eyes off her, Ted pulled a paper from the inside pocket of his jacket and handed it to her. She unfolded it. The letterhead read, "Franklin Auto Repair" under which was written "Car Repair Estimate." Her eyes went directly to the bottom figure and she squirmed slightly as she read, "Total labor and parts $1,450." She looked up at her dinner companion and bit her lower lip like a child who had just committed an embarrassing act.

"I'm not sure I can pay this in one lump sum at this time but if you'll give me a little space I'll be able to handle it. I'm embarrassed to death to say this but last night I called my insurance company only to be told my policy lapsed eight days ago, so I'm on my own on this."

"But Alice"—for the first time that evening he addressed her by her first name—"read the entire paper," he urged as he brought the sherry to his smiling lips.

"What is this, I don't understand, something is wrong here. This says it's an estimate on a 1995 Toyota Camry, why that's my car. It says at the bottom here that the repair cost has been paid in full. Now I'm thoroughly and totally confused. What's this all about, help me out on this." She reached over to hand him the paper and in doing so knocked over her barely sipped glass of sherry. A waiter came scurrying to their table to attend to the spillage.

Rather than responding to her anxious questions, he said he suspected she might question the fact the accident was not her fault as he again reached into his pocket and pulled out a photocopy of some kind of legal looking document.

"This is Section 112 of the Motor Vehicles Law of the State of Virginia which says that cars pulling out from a curb onto the roadway must yield to cars traveling on that roadway. In other words, the accident was my fault and I'm the one who must cover the costs of the damage to your car."

"But," she responded, "it doesn't…"

Interrupting her, he handed her the paper saying he had underlined in red the rule he had just quoted. How did the appraisers know what damage her car had suffered? He gave them a description of her car and they went to the school parking lot and examined it.

Over the next few months the parent and the teacher not only had more dinners together, they went to the movies and exhibitions, cocktail parties and played tennis. Recently, they had gone to bed together, something she had delayed longer than he had anticipated. She needed the conviction that he had not been hitting on her from the start. She required that if it was to happen it would not be out of a sudden urgent surge of whatever, but that it was an honest, natural consequence of their evolving relationship. In this she was conservative.

Lately, she sensed that Ted was on the verge of suggesting they move their relationship to a new level, something more permanent or structured, not necessarily marriage but perhaps living together. If she was reading him correctly he had been dropping inferences here and there. So concerned was she that he might make such a proposal that she had prepared a response in advance.

Moving in together would jeopardize her teaching position if word of it got out, which would be hard to avoid happening. Not that she was particularly enamored of her job but jobs of any kind were not exactly abundant at this time. Moreover, all of this was happening too fast for her. She was not ready to make the type of commitment, limited as it might be, that would be implicit in the proposed living-together arrangement.

As far as marriage was concerned it was definitely out of the question, Ted was kind and considerate, dependable, financially well-off and would probably make someone a good husband, but she was far from convinced she was that someone. She required more fire, more adventurousness, more mystery and creative unpredictability in her man. Then there was the matter of age difference, some 20 years or so. Not a problem up to now but might become one.

She wasn't sure how many of these concerns she should express to Ted Shaw but in the end it didn't matter since he never asked the required question. Not that he hadn't given thought to these ideas, particularly about moving in together. Years ago he would have categorically dismissed such a notion, but times change and with it what is socially acceptable. In his company, for instance, there was a debate going on as to whether an employee's live-in partner can be covered by an employer-sponsored health plan. What really gave him pause was the fact he has always been wary of getting involved in situations whose implications were uncertain. Order, discipline and predictability were at the heart of his ethos. Alice was generations younger than he and had shown a certain propensity for experimenting, trying new things and all that stuff. Then there was his daughter Cindy. No, it would be best to hold off on any thoughts about a closer relationship.

With these thoughts in mind, Ted sought to get Alice involved in activities of interest to him that were new to her, and in the process learn whether she was capable of enjoying his favorite activities and sharing their pleasures with him. An experiment in potential compatibility, or, in his mind, a lessening of the risks of unpredictability.

Tennis was one of the activities Ted had convinced her to participate in. A good tennis player who had been hitting balls over nets since before high school, Ted outfitted Alice with the latest in tennis outfits, sneakers, expensive rackets and an instructor. She proved to be a fast learner, lean and quick, with a good eye for following the ball. Soon they were playing singles together and doubles with Ted's friends.

It was during a trip to New York to attend a U.S. Open Tennis Tournament that Alice brought up the subject of blue people that Ted had mentioned the morning of their parent-teacher session.

"This idea of blue people has captured my imagination," she told Ted, "I've actually done a little research on the subject but haven't found anything."

As part of his efforts to foster their relationship and recalling the interest Alice had shown in the matter, Ted had also looked into it. I've also done a little gumshoe work on this but like you I've come up empty-handed. I wouldn't be surprised if this whole thing is phony, just someone's hallucination. As far as he could recall his Zambillan friend Luis never did reveal the source of his information.

"Did you have the impression Luis was serious in what he told you, I mean did he seem to believe these people existed. As a matter of fact, precisely what did he tell you?"

"As far as I recall Luis was not the type of person who would fabricate a story, he was always a serious straight-up guy. He didn't know much about these alleged blue people, it was all hearsay. I don't even remember how the subject ever came up."

"I suppose it's just the late stirring of my college anthropology classes, but I'm fascinated by this subject."

"Tell you what, I'll write to Luis on this and try to get more information, how does that sound?"

"Could you!"

CHAPTER 2

▼

Chucaya is a moderate size city some 200 miles southeast of Santa Fe, the capitol of Zambilla, and a short distance from the base of the harsh but beautiful Sierra, the country's north-south spinal cord. Thin mountain air, clay red land, river gullies, flowering cactus plants and distant snow covered peaks rise to a dizzying elevation of over 12,000 feet; home to a large number of native Indians; economy predominantly agricultural with beans, corn, potatoes and chili peppers as the mountain produce; religion catholic, socially and, as one would expect, politically conservative.

Chucaya is where Luis Carlos Pradilla publishes his daily newspaper "El Clarin," a respected voice of the region's moderate conservatism, and the city's only daily. Arriving home from work, Luis Carlos went to his study where he found the day's mail on his desk arranged in a neat stack, on the top a letter bearing postage stamps of the United States, the addressee, Mr. Ted Shaw. He picked up the letter, slid a silver letter opener under the top flap, removed the single hand-written sheet and without checking the rest of the mail sat in his favorite alpaca-upholstered reading chair, but not before pouring himself his customary arrival-home glass of scotch.

As he held the letter on his lap, he thought how odd that his old college friend Ted Shaw would write him a letter since over the past few years their correspondence had, almost by tacit agreement, been limited to Christmas salutations. In a way, he regretted it had been so meager. He recalled the long, late night sessions at Boston College where they covered a whole range of subjects. Ted had not been much into studying, feeling turned off by the demands of academic discipline. He claimed he had entered college under the duress of his father's insistence. Yet, he was intelligent in a natural, non-bookish way. How odd it seemed to Luis Carlos to learn that post-graduation Ted Shaw had made a 180-degree reversal to become engaged in the quintessential conservative world of insurance when in college his ideas were clearly of the left. Luis Carlos put on his reading glasses.

My Dear Friend Luis Carlos:

I can imagine your surprise at receiving this letter when for years now my words to you have been confined to holiday greetings. Honesty prevents me from excusing myself by blaming this on the demanding nature of my work, which supposedly left me no time for correspondence. Yet, that same honesty also insists that I tell you that my thoughts about you have not been limited to the holidays, for I often recall those pleasant days we shared at Boston College.

I trust that you continue to enjoy success with your newspaper. Incidentally, I have never received a copy of "El Clarin." Though my Spanish is hardly good enough to guarantee I would understand all that is in the paper, I believe I have picked up enough of the language here and there to get the drift of it. As you are probably aware, an at least passing knowledge of Spanish is fast assuming importance here in the States, especially in matters of commerce and politics.

I am embarrassed by the fact that my first letter to you after so long hiatus is a request for your assistance. You will pardon me for this.

During one of our conversations back in Boston you told me about a tribe or small community of natives of your country that had blue-colored skin. I've forgotten the context in which this came up but it has made a lasting impression on me.

Recently, I met a lovely young lady. Her name is Alice Reddy. We have become close friends, enough so as to cause me to wonder where this may lead. As you can appreciate, the loss of my wife a year ago has left a painful void.

But getting back to the blue-skinned people, I mentioned this to Alice, and she, having majored in anthropology in college, has also become fascinated with this. Her efforts to research the subject have been unrewarding as have mine.

Now to my request. Is it possible you can have someone send us information on these people? Anything at all you can do in this regard will be appreciated by both of us for, as I said, we have uncovered nothing on the subject at this end.

In the hope that this letter finds you in good health and that it heralds the start of renewed correspondence between us, I remain you admiring friend.

Abrazos
Ted Shaw"

Some 10 days later Ted Shaw received a letter postmarked Chucaya, Zambilla.

My Very Dear Friend Ted:

How wonderful to receive your letter. You have no cause to be embarrassed for not writing to me as I am equally at fault.

What good news you give me about your new friend Alice Reddy. I sincerely hope things work out so that the emptiness of your loss will to some extent be filled with a new joy.

Now to your request. What I told you about the blue skin people had its source in what I believe you call *hearsay* and anecdotal comments of people (you see, I do remember some of the Americanisms I learned in Boston). To the best of my knowledge there has never been a serious study or investigation of this. However, a pleasant thought has occurred to me. Would you and Miss Reddy do me the honor of accepting an invitation to stay with me this coming summer? While you are here you can talk to people about this subject of blue people. As a matter of fact, I have a dear friend Maria Isabel Montavo who has information that may be useful to you. I might even arrange for someone to take you to a general area where these people were reported to have been seen, with the warning that the location is said to be somewhere high in the Sierras which are only a few kilometers from here. There are places in these mountains that are over 12,000 feet above sea level.

Please give this serious consideration. For my part it would be a pleasure to have you here, to meet Ms. Reddy, and to enjoy the opportunity of seeing you again and revisiting some of the subjects we discussed during our bull sessions.

Your Friend,
Luis Carlos

*   *   *   *

Three months later Ted Shaw and Alice Reddy are sitting in a restaurant at the Miami International Airport.

"Wow, this is strong," said a surprised Ted Shaw as he pushed the demi-tasse of Cuban coffee back to Alice's side of the table and reached for his glass of water. "That takes some getting used to, the amount of caffeine in this coffee must be measured in metric tons. I suppose Cubans don't drink this stuff at night or it would be *adios* to sleep."

The coffee had been ordered by Alice who had never tasted it before and was curious with inquisitiveness much in tune with her penchant for opening herself up to new experiences. She told Ted that though she wasn't exactly excited about the coffee, she could drink it.

"I like trying new things," she explained.

Ted suggested tongue-in-check that she might want to try a Cuban cigar since she had never tried one of those either, had she?

"Very funny," exclaimed Alice, "but you know, I would even do that if they weren't so big and fat."

"You restless adventurer," whispered Ted as he reached over and kissed her on her cheek. Then he got up and said he was going to the men's room.

The reference to restless adventurer shook her memory tree.

The earliest manifestation of Alice Reddy's propensity for risky adventure she could remember was back to when she was around ten. After a heavy snowfall, she decided to race automobiles down Birch Road on her sled and ended up in the hedges in front of the Hodges house with a bruised nose. A few years later, she managed to convince her parents to let her go bungee jumping in lieu of the senior prom. And how could she ever forget the first semester of her junior year in college that she spent in southern Italy in an archeological studies program jointly sponsored by the University of Palermo and Fordham University. Having become interested in the Israeli-Palestinian conflict and disappointed with what she believed was skewed reporting by the mass media, she decided to get what she hoped would be the true story by going to Israel. During the week she was there she accepted an invitation to go to a club in Jerusalem. Her date was late in picking her up. While on their way to the club a Palestinian suicide bomber reduced the place to rubble.

Alice had recently engaged in some self-analyzing and concluded that her penchant for new experiences was symptomatic of something deeper than mere curiosity. It had more to do with what she felt was her inability to find any direction to her life. She was unsure of what she wanted from life, if anything at all, and attributed her adventurousness to an attempt to find an answer.

Her relationship with Ted and the different life-style that came with it, probably fell into that search category, aided and abetted by the fact she was unhappy and disinterested in her role as a teacher.

She was reminded of a comment made by a young psychologist she had dated for a while who had the annoying habit of making analytical comments about everyone he knew. Jazmin was paranoid, Peter was schizophrenic, Larry was a manic-depressive etcetera, etcetera, etcetera. As to Alice, his unsolicited prognosis was that she had an incipient case of existential crisis.

She had no idea what he meant, nor did his attempt to explain make it any more understandable. One thing was for sure, it didn't sound like something she would want to go around bragging about.

She took another sip of Cuban coffee. A herd of people passed by obediently following a girl holding up a placard reading, "Carnival Cruises Bahamas," Ted was standing on the other side waiting for the happy voyagers to pass.

"I would guess at least 80% or even more of the people who work at this airport are Hispanics," observed Ted as he sat down. "Don't you get the feeling we're already in a foreign country?"

"Actually, it's a good warm-up to our visit to Zambilla, kind of helps the ear to get accustomed to hearing Spanish spoken," pointed out Alice. "By the way, did I give you my ticket?"

Ted pulled two plane tickets from his jacket pocket. "Here you are, Alice Reddy, Zambilla Airlines, destination Santa Fe, connecting Andes Airlines Flight # 701 to Chucaya. I suppose we should head for the departure gate. Do you need any reading material?"

CHAPTER 3

▼

Her religious name was Sister Dolores of St. Francis. On her birth certificate issued in Ghent, Belgium her name appears as Dianna Claus daughter of Louis de Claus and Charloria Guamart. Sister Dolores was short and her back seriously arched. From a childhood sickness the muscles of the upper reaches of her arms from the elbows to her shoulders had atrophied, leaving little more than skin-covered bone. While her hair was sparse and thin, the features of her very attractive face were beautifully proportioned. Her head, however, was so large it gave the impression it was intended for a different body than the one it was attached to.

Her father was a Lutheran minister and she, the only child of the marriage, was initiated into that faith. Despite the religious ambience of her home and the indulgences of which she was beneficiary, she exhibited a growing coldness towards her parents that at times bordered on bitterness. A psychologist familiar with the situation gave the easy opinion that her attitude was due to what she subconsciously felt was the culpability of her parents for her abnormal physical appearance. Towards her classmates, she was defensively aloof, but also quick to denigrate those who she thought were ridiculing her. Paradoxically, there was clearly a deep strain of spirituality in Dianna, as if two personalities roamed her body vying for dominance.

Upon reaching her twentieth birthday and with no forewarning, she left home and went to Italy where she converted to Catholicism, simultaneously entering a novitiate where she underwent preparation for becoming a nun of the Benedictine Order. Interpreting her conversion as an *ad hominen* blow directed at him, the minister father severed all ties with his daughter.

Over the years Sister Dolores cultivated a reputation as a good administrator and strict disciplinarian. Though not devoid of the expected pieties of a good nun, these were overshadowed by her organizational flair. Not lost on her was the fact that becoming a nun had also provided her with the opportunity to cloak her physical anomalies beneath her religious habit.

Two years after arriving at the Convent in Chucaya—a transfer she had personally sought—she was made prioress. Upon the death of the abbess three years later, she was promoted to that position, the highest in the Convent.

Father Manfredo de la Oz first saw the light of day in Cordoba, Spain, scion of a socially well-positioned family whose prominence went back many generations. As was often the case with children of his family's status, he was first educated in an ecclesiastical boarding school where it become obvious early on that he was precociously brilliant. Unlike the majority of the students, he continued on the religious path, first as an undergraduate seminary student and later as a Jesuit novice. His first parish assignment was in Spain where he was a rapid learner. There were early signs that he would be better fulfilled and effective as a parish priest than as a theologian or teacher fettered to some university or other center of learning.

Ten years following his becoming a novice he was transferred from Spain to the parish of the Church of the Sacred Heart in San Jose, Zambilla where he remained for three years before being sent to replace retiring Father Roberto of the Saint Anthony Church in Chucaya. On one point there was unanimity of opinion among the parishioners of Saint Anthony. Father Manfredo had the dazzling gift of eloquence, which when combined with the deep richness of his voice, produced thunderous sermons that kept the parishioners transfixed and hanging on each phrase.

The priest seemed to have all that a man, if not one of the cloths, could wish for within the context of a Latin perspective. His eyes were dark and large, under his biretta, which he seldom removed, there was an abundance of dark wavy hair below which his forehead rose high and his nose assumed a Patrician character.

As if these attractive features were not enough, the priest had the social graces of elegant manners and engaging conversation. It was said he could turn a compliment with easy grace and that if the recipient was a woman, the look that accompanied his words was more flattering than the words themselves.

But it was his very popularity among the women that made him equally unpopular among the men. Husbands and fathers were suspicious and wary of this suave, clever dandy with his genteel manners. There was a general perception among them that his interest in the female parishioners went beyond the merely pastoral. Though no one could point to any actual indiscretions on his part, there was a general feeling of bemused uneasiness about him. Some wished he would be caught in a scandalous act so he could be pilloried and their suspicious vindicated.

*   *   *   *

"Señor, we are sorry but the flight to Chucaya has been cancelled for today," said the harassed, perspiring Andes Airline representative at the airport in Santa Fé.

"Do you mean it's delayed, you know what I mean it's late, you know, late," asked Ted Shaw.

"No, señor there will be no flight today."

"But we have tickets for today's 2 :00 flight, look here, flight # 701, Santa Fé to Chucaya." These words were left floating like bubbles in the air as the airline representative walked away to attend to others. At the airline counter Ted was told that the cancelled flight would leave the next day at 11:15 am, guaranteed.

"What a great beginning this is, hope it's not an omen of what's to come," said flustered Ted Shaw.

"This is certainly not the first experience I would have wished for you in our country," apologized the voice at the other end of the line, "but do not worry, we have an office in Santa Fe and I shall arrange for you to be driven here, if you do not mind coming by land. It will give you an opportunity to see how beautiful our country is, unless, of course, you wish to spend a night in Santa Fé."

"That's really thoughtful of you Luis Carlos," responded Ted Shaw, "but I'm afraid I am already imposing on your generosity."

As he was saying this Alice was motioning to Ted and forming silent words on her lips. Realizing Ted did not understand, she whispered in his ear, "Let's stay over here in Santa Fé tonight, we can see what night-life is like and maybe find a good restaurant."

"No, no, it is I who must apologize for the way you have been greeted in my country, our local airline has much to learn from those in your country," continued Luis Carlos.

Before Ted could respond to Luis' proposal a youngster tried to wrest Alice's handbag from her. Ted, while continuing to hold on to the phone, kicked the thief in the stomach. The would-be purse-snatcher instantly let go of the handbag and ran down the corridor rubbing his pain. Turning to Alice, "are you alright? Guess that settles it about staying here overnight, let's just get the hell out of here, this place is dangerous."

Within 45 minutes Ted Shaw and Alice Reddy were seated in a white station wagon with the words "El Clarin" written on both sides heading southeast, towards Chucaya.

*   *   *   *

On a sizeable tract of land enclosed on three sides by richly foliaged trees, cattle were languidly grazing in the afternoon gray as the white station wagon passed by headed for a stone farmhouse at the end of the lane where Luis Carlos' Indian maid Inga awaited them. She was soon joined by a youngster who took the Americans' bags into the house.

The lady spoke only Spanish, but by pooling their combined, limited understanding of the language the couple understood that the Americanos were expected, that Luis Carlos was sorry he could not be there to greet them, that he would arrive shortly, and that they should follow her to their room. Ted appreciated the fact they would have a chance of freshen-up and rest before seeing Luis Carlos.

No sooner had their bags touched the floor when the room phone rang. It was Luis Carlos calling to check on them and to apologize for not being there at their arrival, last minute matters requiring his attention prevented him from doing so. They would have a quiet dinner at home this evening.

Dinner, to which Luis Carlos had invited his friend Maria Isabel Montavo was served on the house patio. The evening was pleasantly cool and the food spicy. Neither of the Americans had ever tasted such exotic dishes as were served that evening, except for Ted who once tried the universally popular *cebiche* in Boston at Luis Carlos' invitation. Alice was so delighted that she wrote down the names of some of the dishes, Pika Picante, Anticucho y Picarones, Aji de Gallina and Papa a la Huancaina.

Luis proved to be an engaging host, but definitely not the physical stereotype Latin Alice had anticipated. There was no tan, no slim figure, no dark romantic eyes with hair to match. The man Ted introduced to her stood a moderate 5'9" with a body that apparently had not seen the inside of a gym for years; blonde hair which he kept in a style reminding her somewhat of a fading Robert Redford; a nose slightly flattish and greenish gray eyes. All in all, hardly the portrait that Alice realized she had artlessly sketched of an educated, rich, charming, suave and sophisticated Latin American, or was she confusing the image with that of a Spanish toreador. Ted commented during dinner that Luis had hardly changed at all from his university days in Boston.

Maria Isabel Montavo, Luis called her "Marisa" spoke little during the course of dinner, though it was obvious she too had an excellent command of English. When she did speak it was mostly the result of Luis having eased her into the conversation by asking her to confirm something he had said, or, when the subject was Zambillan history, to help him fill in the blank spots of his recollection.

Marisa's physiognomy left little doubt about her native Indian roots: her hair was long, straight and lustrous black, cheekbones high, her nose slightly eagle-like imperial, and a hint of the oriental in her eyes. Her body was slim, her complexion semi-dark, skin tight, clear and unblemished. What caught Alice's attention in particular were Marisa's hands, not so much their shape but the gracefulness of their movements—it was later that Alice learned she was a sculptor. Alice had the impression there was a latent fire and energy in Marisa's body. Luis did not explain their relationship beyond saying she was a dear friend. Alice concluded she wanted to know more about Luis' friend.

These observations by Alice during the course of dinner fueled the excitement she felt at being there in Zambilla and by what she intuitively knew awaited her. Ted's attention was taken up by the topics of the polite dinner conversation, except for the quick passing thought that women with broad foreheads like Marisa's struck him as being sensual, which in his mind probably explained why Luis had this Indian girl as a friend.

Following dinner, Luis suggested they go to his library for a brandy or liqueur and see a video he had taken in Boston which he had dug up in anticipation of Ted's visit.

The video proved to be of amateurish quality, containing bouncing scenes of the B.C. campus, Fenway Park, the Commons, the Science Museum and the Italian North End. Ted appeared briefly in a few of them. In the shots taken at the Science Museum a girl who later became Mrs. Shaw appeared. She was a student at Boston University at that time.

While Ted had not changed much beyond what the imprint of the intervening years could be expected to reveal, Luis, on the other hand, was appreciably trimmer than now which belied Ted's earlier comment about Luis not having changed much since their college days.

Luis commented that his daily exposure to Americans outside the academic world was as much a part of his learning experience as were the textbooks and lectures. Alice wanted to know what he came away with from his four years in Boston.

"Probably how much liquor American college students could consume in one evening," joked Ted.

Luis laughed and said he seemed to remember that the amount was unlimited. Put out by what she thought was Ted's lame attempt at humor, Alice repeated her question.

Luis reached over for his glass of brandy, took a sip, then putting the glass back on the table said, "admiration tempered by a disquieting concern." The admiration was over the huge technical and materialistic accomplishments that America had made in so many areas, which he attributed to the deep-seated individualism of Americans, one that was fueled by a powerful drive to experiment and innovate.

Ted commented that that was how the American West was won. Alice added that this character trait was often said to be the result of the so-called Protestant work ethic combined by the fact that during the country's years of westward expansion the vastness of the American territory guaranteed that there would be abundant terrain between those who first settled the country, in turn compelling individuals to resort to their own wits, all of which became hardwired into the country's ethos. She pointed out that during the very late 19th and early 20th centuries waves of immigrants from Europe recharged the country's vitality.

Realizing she was giving a speech, she turned to Luis, "If this was the object of your admiration then what was the disquieting concern you mentioned?"

"I had the sensation that individualism carried to an extreme could lead to dangerous self-absorption and a disconnect from the wider world, a lessening of interest, concern and compassion for others. I recall reading your great writer Ralph Waldo Emerson and how he eloquently argued the case for individualism, but also how he bitterly opposed giving charity and was against Americans touring foreign countries because they had all they needed right in their own backyard. This is the danger I saw lurking in unbridled individualism. The recent scandals in corporate America involving company executives who have defrauded stockholders and amassed huge fortunes give evidence of what I am talking about. Uncontrolled individualism may sometimes contain elements of greed which if allowed to germinate will in the end pollute the very source of the country's success."

Luis' comments dissipated a part of the wine-induced mellowness from Ted's mind, and replaced it with a call to national defense. He proclaimed that the number of corrupt executives is very limited, and that the business world was ethically very sound, after all, he was a corporate executive and should know.

Surprised by Ted's testy outburst, Luis politely explained that he was certainly in agreement with Ted and that what he intended to convey was simply an example of where rampant individualism could lead.

Realizing the conversation had taken a wrong turn, Marisa said she understood Alice had expressed interest in the so-called blue people. Luis interjected that Marisa probably knew more about the subject than anyone else.

"Great," enthused Alice, "I'm fascinated by this, I would love to hear what you know about these people, you see, I majored in anthropology in college."

Luis suggested they have coffee, a suggestion Marisa was quick to endorse for, "it was brewed from Luis' own special blend of rare Latin American beans."

Wanting to be closer to the source of the information she had been longing to hear, and so as to not miss a word of it, Alice moved her chair closer to Marisa. Ted remained seated back in his chair, still smarting from the inferences he thought ought to be drawn from Luis' comments about business executives. Luis exhibited the relaxation of someone who was about to hear a familiar story.

Stories about a group of people with blue skin who live in the Sierra had been around for some time, opened Marisa. But since no one claimed to have actually seen them, nor did anyone know for sure how the stories started, they were relegated to the status of myths or legends. But the idea of such people captured Marisa's curiosity and led her to attempt to trace the stories to some concrete indication of their veracity.

Anecdotal reports led her to a man known only as *Mr. Charlie*. She succeeded in tracking him down to an address in a neighboring town. He had no listed phone so Marisa went to the address she had been given. There was no one at home. His neighbors told her Mr. Charlie was not Zambillan but Greek and that he spoke good Spanish. He didn't socialize at all with his neighbors and spent a lot of time in the Sierra, where he was believed to be at that time. He had some kind of business or other involving animals. His best friend was a guy called Jesus Camargo who lived across town.

Jesus did have a phone but it took three calls to convince him to meet with Marisa. She found Jesus to be a nervous, edgy person who insisted in making two things clear from the start; one, he personally had never seen any blue skinned people, and two, Charlie—whose last name was Theoros—was not the type of person who would lie.

Marisa turned to Ted and Alice and said she realized they had had a long day of travel and events and that if at any point they preferred she suspend her account of what happened, they should feel no compunction in telling her so. She could continue tomorrow or the day after, or whenever they desired.

"I'll stay up all night to hear this," quickly responded Alice, "I think Ted will also."

"I'm with you," said Ted.

Charlie was in the business of tracking down and capturing exotic animals and exporting them out of the country. Originally, the animals were from the Zambillan rainforest and more recently from the Sierra. Jesus occasionally accompanied Charlie on his hunting expeditions.

Some six months earlier they had gone into the Sierra.

"I'm sorry to interrupt you but when did all of this happen," asked Alice.

"My meeting with Jesus happened about a year ago."

"Sorry, please go on."

"On that particular trip they were having little success in the areas frequented by them, so they decided to climb to a higher elevation. After a while, Jesus felt ill and decided to head back. He convinced Mr. Charlie to continue on and not to worry about him for he would be alright once he got to a lower elevation. It was expensive and took time to prepare for these expeditions and it made no sense to abort this one. Three days later Mr. Charlie was back in town, exhausted and literally bursting with excitement.

"Now what I'm about to relate is what Mr. Charlie told Jesus so what you are about to hear is what someone told me about what someone told him. You will be three layers away from what allegedly happened," clarified Marisa.

"We understand, please continue."

"After Jesus turned back, Charlie continued his slow and arduous trek up the now inhospitable mountain. After a couple of luckless hours he was about to change directions when he noticed a path had been opened through the bush. Believing it might have been made by animals, he followed it to a formation of boulders which he proceeded to climb. Reaching the top, he found himself facing a clearing and a series of makeshift huts, but no signs of life.

"Curious, he took a few steps down toward the clearing when a loose rock he was stepping on gave way and rolled down towards the clearing and in the process dislodged other rocks.

"People came out of the huts and he was quickly spotted. They gathered in the center of the clearing whispering to each other with eyes fixed on Mr. Charlie. Unable to think of anything else to do, he waived at the group and shouted out that he was hunting animals, had they seen any. Eliciting no response and anticipating the worse as the group edged closer, he thought it best to back away from the place as nonchalantly as possible. As he turned to do so, he found himself face to face with two men dressed in the same heavy poncho-like garment and woolen cap with earflaps worn by those in the clearing. They spoke to him in words he had never before heard, not at all like the Quechua spoken by the country's indigenous natives. Charlie repeated he was looking for rare animals.

"The men frowned and pointed down to the clearing as they advanced closer to him, leaving no doubt as to what they wanted him to do.

"In the clearing, the group formed a circle around him. One of the men who had ordered him down and who seemed to be a leader, took Charlie's backpack and emptied it item by item, examining each and then handing it to his companion who after examining it, tossed it at Charlie's feet. When all of the items lay on the ground, the group dissolved the circle and went to the pile and began handing the items around.

"While this was happening Mr. Charlie noticed with wide-eyed astonishment that the presumed leader's skin was turning blue. First his face, then his neck and hands. Charlie turned to the others as if to say, look, someone help him, only to see that the same thing was happening to them, as if they were reacting to an inaudible signal or were in someway connected to the leader. Blueness was sweeping over them like a wave. No one gave a sign of having noticed or being surprised by what was happening. Later, he recalled that as they turned blue all talk ceased and their physical movements slowed down almost as if they had switched to slow motion.

"Charlie thought he was dreaming. He closed his eyes and rubbed them for a moment. When he opened them an elderly woman was standing in front of him holding an earthen vessel in her extended blue hands. She did not speak. He could see it contained a liquid. Concerned it might be dangerous yet not wanting to antagonize these strange creatures, he accepted the cup, took a whiff of the contents and then a sip. It had a hint of sharp ginger to it. The woman urged him to drink more. As he raised the vessel to his lips and looked into her face, he saw that her eyes were the same blue as her skin, making them practically indistinguishable from the rest of her face. This sent a chill throbbing down his back. No sooner had he taken a larger swallow when the chill was replaced by a burning sensation that started in his face and then swept down his body. He thought he had been poisoned. The sensation lasted about a minute or so.

The people seemed to lose interest in Mr. Charlie and his backpack contents and in slow-motion languidness walked away leaving him standing there. Taking this as a sign that it was okay to exit the scene, he hurriedly filled his backpack, smiled sheepishly at anyone looking in his direction, and headed towards the rock formation, but before reaching there the world began to spin. Someone then pulled the shades down and all was darkness.

"It was cold when he opened his eyes. It took a few moments to reassemble his thoughts and recall what had happened. It seemed like early morning. He was lying in the middle of the clearing. Looking around he saw nothing that once was there, no huts, no people, only an empty clearing. Had he been dreaming? Walking around he found no evidence of anyone having been there, not even ashes from the fires which had given off the smoke he had seen coming from the huts the day before.

"He followed a path out of the clearing to a plateau which led to even higher elevations, most of which were shrouded in early morning fog."

Marisa stopped speaking. There was silence in the room which Ted broke with a "Wow, what a story," did Marisa believe it really happened. She said she wasn't sure at that time but she did want to relate the last part of the story.

"Sorry, I thought you had finished."

"Mr. Charlie told Jesus he had just come up with a great idea. He knew people would doubt the truth of his encounter, so he would present them with irrefutable evidence. Suppose he could locate these people again and bring one of them back with him. He could make a fortune on this, more than he could by selling exotic animals. Jesus was skeptical. How would he manage to convince one of the blue people to go with him, or did he have something else in mind. Mr. Charlie didn't know at the moment. Should he not be able to bring a live body back, he intended to do the second best, he would film the group and record their voices.

"A few months later, Mr. Charlie went back into the mountains alone, he felt Jesus' presence might cause the blue people to feel threatened. As far as Marisa knew he has not been heard from since."

What did Jesus believe could have happened to his friend, are there dangerous animals up there, hasn't anyone attempted to find him, segued Alice. Ted asked Marisa if she honestly believed there were blue-skin people up there. Couldn't what this Greek saw have been a hallucination. Maybe he had chewed coca leaves. He had read somewhere that Indians who live at high altitudes chew that stuff.

"I expected you to have plenty of questions, smiled Marisa. Now there's a sort of epilogue to this story, but before I get to that, I will try to answer some of your questions. First of all, you should bear in mind that at the higher elevations the Sierra—which I've been assuming you know are part of the Andes—while breathtakingly beautiful and splendid, is also hostile to human life, with its bitter cold, rugged terrain, and raging streams. So it is no surprise that occasionally a brave soul who ventures there is never heard from again. Of course, no one knows how far up Mr. Charlie went or whether he went there at all.

"It was reported that an official search team had gone looking for him, but Jesus doubts this because Charlie's trade in exotic animals, some of which were considered endangered species, had become an embarrassment to the national government. It had been under pressure from foreign governments and international organizations to put an end to this trading. Mr. Charlie avoided being shut down only because he had a godfather in the government who was pocketing money from the business. Jesus was sure Charlie's disappearance caused no official tears to be shed in Santa Fé."

Luis suggested Marisa take a break and rest her vocal cords a while. While the others walked around the room stretching their legs, Luis was on the phone as he had been twice during the talk. Marisa looked over at him with a touch of concern in her eyes. After a couple of minutes Marisa turned to the Americans and said she was ready if they were. Luis hung up the office phone, picked up his cell phone and stepped out of the room. Marisa began, but this time without the enthusiasm and feeling of the engrossing storyteller of minutes earlier.

Unable to find convincing evidence of the truth of what Mr. Charlie had reported, Marisa said she decided to turn to objective science. At the local university's medical school, she posed the questions of whether it was possible that a person could have blue skin, and whether there were any reported cases of this in medical history. She was told there is a condition called cyanosis which occurs when there is a decrease of oxygen to the tissues of an organ, the skin for example. When circulating blood contains adequate oxygen it appears red but turns bluish when it loses the oxygen. The blueness is easily seen in the beds of fingernails and toenails, on the lips and tongue. This condition could be caused by a number of situations including high altitudes where the air is thinner in oxygen.

"But wait a minute," interjected Ted, "lots of people climb mountains to altitudes higher than where this Mr. Charlie went, and they don't blue."

"You're asking the same question I asked. Now it gets a little technical but as I understood it, and I will be glad to introduce you to the people I spoke to if you want a more detailed, first-hand explanation, the red blood cells carry oxygen from the lungs to the organs of the body. Hemoglobin is a molecule in the cells which because of certain conditions in the lungs is able to grab the oxygen and then release it into the different organs where it is used as body fuel. If the molecule becomes defective or for some other reason is unable to take in the necessary amount of oxygen from the lungs, then the body's organs, such as the skin, will be deprived. So what these people were hypothesizing came down to this: high altitude + defective hemoglobin = blue skin."

"But according to what this Mr. Charlie said, the people he saw turned blue before his eyes, they were not blue at first," said Alice.

"Again, I asked the very same question," said Marisa. "What I was told—and I must repeat this was posited as mere speculation—was that these people's bodies could have developed a compensating response-mechanism to the oxygen deficiency which functioned successfully up to a certain point. But when that threshold was crossed, say, for example, when the body suddenly needed an extra boost of oxygen because of physical exertion, distress, or panic, the body's adjustment system could have become overwhelmed. In that case, blueness could result. As a second line of defense and in an effort to stave off death, the body would go into a homeostasis or a compensating low gear, a slowing down, thus reducing its need for oxygen. But the University people were emphatic in pointing out they had never heard of such an acute case of cyanosis. Theoretically possible, though no such extreme case has ever been reported."

"But," interjected Alice, "how is it possible that a whole group of people can suffer from the same condition at the same instant."

"Whatever caused the abnormality could, over time, have become part of their genetic structure, in-breeding would have perpetuated the phenomenon. Now Ted, I want to go back to something you intimated a few moments ago. I am referring to linking the chewing of coca leaves to the possibility that what Mr. Charlie saw was not blue skinned people at all but a hallucination. This is an example of the general misconception out there that confuses coca with the drug cocaine," observed Marisa.

"But cocaine comes from coca leaves."

"You're right, the coca leaf does contain the alkaloid cocaine, but did you know it's only present in an amount that ranges from one to eight tenths of one percent, nowhere near enough to produce the effects you had in mind, unless Mr. Charlie chewed a whole field of leaves.

"Coca has played an important role in our native culture here in Zambilla, as it has in our neighboring countries. This goes back thousands of years, as a matter of fact, and Alice this will interest you, there is archeological evidence that its use goes back as far as 5,000 years. The leaves of the coca plant have an amazing number of beneficial uses. For example, it was and continues to be used for our natives and others for medicinal purposes such as to relieve headaches, muscle aches, arthritis pains and digestive problems.

"It is also used as an energy stimulant by natives who otherwise would be unable to perform the arduous labor they do under extremely hostile climatic conditions. The leaf is an excellent source of nutrients including many vitamins and minerals. This has made it a critical element in the dietary regime of many poor people who live in remote altiplanos, who would otherwise find themselves in dire nutritional condition.

"I should not neglect to mention that coca has played an important role in the spiritual practices of our native population. Coca leaves are one of the components of the sacrificial bundles that are burned as offerings to the gods Pacha Mama (Mother Earth) and Inti (Sun God)."

At this point Marisa checked herself from going any further and instead apologized for lecturing. What she was about to add but didn't was a comment, which she felt might raise Ted's defensive ire, as had Luis' generic comment about corporate executives.

What remained unexpressed by Marisa was what she considered the Mother of all ironies. The fact that the self-styled developed countries had taken an almost sacred product of her native culture, processed it so as to extract one of its ingredients, converted that ingredient into a potent drug which was then used for dangerous recreational purposes.

As the consumption of the processed product became widespread so did the information of its parallel disastrous personal and social effects. And so pressure was exerted on Zambilla to destroy its coca plants and with it an integral part of the culture of its natives.

Marisa recalled her Indian friend Isodoro who was taken to railing against the Europeans' ravaging of Zambilla's native culture. He saw this coca/cocaine issue as a neo-colonial twentieth century effort by foreigners to complete the destruction of Zambilla's native culture.

At that moment Luis re-entered the room. It was obvious to Marisa that something was troubling him. When asked if there was anything wrong, he smiled unconvincingly and said that such a lovely and interesting evening should not be dampened by business matters. He poured everyone a glass of sherry. The four late-nighters raised their glasses to each other and toasted the evening. While Alice's mind was whirling with possibilities and Ted's was dismissive, Luis and Marisa's eyes met and Marisa knew something had happened. A few minutes later when Marisa was about to leave, Alice asked whether it would be possible to meet Mr. Charlie's friend Jesus. She would see what she could do.

Later that evening in their room, Ted expressed his displeasure with the sour events that had occurred since their arrival in Zambilla. The airport incident, Luis' attack on American corporate executives and then the dressing down on his innocent reference to coca leaves.

Alice was of a different mind. Purses were also stolen in the U.S., the reference to executive greed was only an example and it did exist, present company excluded. As to coca leaves, Marisa merely corrected Ted on a widespread misunderstanding in the nature and cultural truth about the plant; her condemnation of efforts to eradicate the plant was definitely on the mark and at minimum a fact that must be kept in mind.

"You may be right but I am not convinced," answered Ted. "In any event, I hope this day is not a harbinger of what lies ahead." Alice remained silent but thought she liked the feeling she sensed of a certain edginess in the air as suggested by their experiences so far in Zambilla.

At Luis Carlos' suggestion, Ted and Alice spent the following day relaxing from the previous day's travel fatigue.

CHAPTER 4

▼

When Ted went down for breakfast on the second day, he was handed a note from Luis Carlos saying he had urgent matters to attend to at *El Clarin*, and apologized for not having breakfast with him and Alice. Marisa planned to pick them up at around ten for their first tour of the city. He would join them later for lunch.

Marisa arrived early and had a cup of coffee with the Americans. She said she tried to call Jesus Camargo but there was no answer. Alice said she had a restless first night. The blue people matter kept her thinking and wondering.

As they drove through the city on their way to a museum, Marisa felt something unusual in the air, a kind of hovering expectancy. She was concerned for she knew too well her uncanny ability to sense a disturbance of what she describes as the normal flow of energy around her. Nothing she saw this morning appeared to be different, except for an unusual number of cars with license plates from other provinces. Not wanting to give the Americans anything to worry about, she kept her feelings to herself.

Though he courteously indicated that his visit to the Museo de Antiguedades Indigenas had been interesting, the truth is that Ted was bored. He was never big on still art. One exception was the WOW! Disney World-like introduction to the museum when, standing in the center of a pitch-black room, spotlights suddenly illuminated previously curtained gold artifacts surrounding them, suffusing the room in the radiance of a skin-tingling golden light.

Alice felt she had entered the temple of an ancient Inca culture. Greeted by monoliths and colonial vitrified jars and vases, they walked through rooms arranged to convey the chronology of Zambillan societies as expressed in their artifacts, beginning with the Pre-ceramic, the Hunters and Fishers to the arrival of the Spaniards. Pottery, metal, wood, textiles, gold and silver work were all represented. There was even a collection of erotic pottery which Doctor Kinsey, the renowned sexologist, was reported to have said was extraordinary.

Alice loved the museum and hoped to go through it again before leaving the country.

The Rincon de Toledo was the rustic restaurant where, according to Marisa, genius Chef Antonio created wonderfully imaginative dishes. When the trio got there Luis Carlos had not yet arrived but he had reserved a table. Alice was commenting on the things that impressed her in the museum and a trio of guitar players began warming up in a corner when the owner of the restaurant, Wilfredo, came to their table to greet Marisa. She told him she noticed an unusual number of foreigners in the restaurant, was there an international convention of some kind, which would be extraordinarily unusual for Chucaya.

No, there was no convention, as far as he could tell these guys were foreign reporters. Whatever their reason for being there, they were welcome, they were good customers with generous expense accounts and that was what mattered.

The guitarists strolled over to their table and asked for requests.

"They won't know any of my songs," dismissed Alice.

Marisa turned to Ted with a *and you look*.

"Ted, maybe they know one of Diana Krall's numbers," jokingly suggested Alice.

"Diana who?"

"Diana Krall."

"I've never heard of her, who is she?"

"You haven't?" Remember the first night you called me, the night you asked me out to dinner to discuss our car accident."

"Of course I do, how could I forget, but what does that have to do with this Diana Krall person?"

"That evening you were playing one of her CDs, I could hear it in the background. I don't remember the song she was singing."

"I've never owned any CDs, I must have had my radio on. Who is she anyway? Should I have heard of her?"

"It doesn't really matter. Look, these gentlemen are waiting for you to name a song."

"My mother just loved Latin music, she could listen to it all day long. One of her favorites was, let me see if I can remember. Oh, yes, it was *You Belong To My Heart*, how could I ever forget.

The trio didn't recognize the title even in its translation, albeit literal, could he sing or hum the melody.

"Well I'm not very good at this but it goes something like this…"

"Solamente Una Vez," said Marisa as the trio picked up the melody. That's a very romantic song you remembered," as she smiled at Alice.

But Alice's thoughts were still with the fact that Ted never even knew who Diana Krall was. Ridiculous, but she felt she had been taken.

Luis Carlos arrived and quietly slipped into a chair so as not to interrupt the private serenade. When the singers finished and Luis had a tipped them, they headed for a corner table where a young couple were holding hands and looking into each other's eyes while the ice in their hardly touched drinks was dissolving away.

"Sorry about rushing off this morning but I'm consoled by the fact you have been in good hands," apologized Luis to his American guests.

"Marisa has been just great," beamed Alice.

"You are calling her Marisa, that is good, it tells me you have hit it off well," observed Luis Carlos. Now you may call me Luis.

A waiter came to the table to tell Luis that one of the gentlemen at the table across the room, who he pointed out by head motion, wanted to have a word with him and sent his personal card. Luis looked at the card, "Tony Glassmore, reporter British Broadcasting Corporation (BBC), Santa Fé." Tell Mr. Glassmore if he wants to see me he should go to my office and not disturb my lunch. Turning to the others at his table, he expressed an irritated surprise that the famously polite English would be so rude, but they were more surprised by Luis' uncharacteristically harsh response.

Marisa turned her gaze from Luis to the table across the room and then back to Luis. "Luis, what's happening in this city, there's something strange going on, what is it, I've got the feeling you know what it is?"

He sat pensively for a moment, then with a touch of resignation in his voice said, "All right, this will become public fairly soon in any event, but let us move away from here to a more private area," as he called a waiter and said they wanted to move to one of the private dining rooms.

Once they had moved Luis began. "What I am about to tell you is all that I know about this matter. Though there's no way word about this will not soon be public, in the meantime I ask that what I tell you here in this room not be discussed with anyone else."

The three agreed though Ted wondered who Alice and he could discuss it with since the only people they knew in the country were Luis and Marisa.

"Three nights ago one of El Clarin's reporters was returning home from work when he passed the Bishop's residence and saw a police car pull up in front of it. His curiosity aroused, he turned his car around. Two police officers emerged from the car and from the back seat a nun with her habit in disarray. The three entered the residence, the nun between the officers. Wondering what this was all about, the reporter parked his car and waited.

"Thirty or so minutes later the officers emerged. The reporter knew both of them. As they were about to drive away, he pulled up next to their car. Telling them what he had seen, he asked what had happened. At first they were closed to any explanation but under the pressure of his insistence and fearing what he might otherwise report in his paper, they agreed to speak, but only if it would be kept off-the-record, which he agreed to. They said that they found a nun running down Avenida Patriota as if she were being pursued. When they caught up with her they saw she was distraught, but all they could get from her was that she "had to tell the Bishop" and that "only he could help." They drove her to the Bishop's residence, which is when the reporter saw them.

"The officers refused to divulge any information about what had happened inside the residence, it was part of the police report. They did say the nun was from the Convent."

Alice asked Marisa if that is the same convent they were supposed to visit that afternoon. She said it was, everyone referred to it simply as the Convent.

Luis continued. "The reporter, sensing something unusual had happened, decided to park near the residence. Shortly, his hunch seemed to bear fruit as a number of clergy and others arrived. Hoping there was a story behind all this activity, he knocked at the residence door and showed his official press ID. He was told regular office hours were from 10-4. As he was about to open his mouth to speak, he found himself facing a closed door.

The following morning the reporter informed Luis of the incident. Luis told him to discontinue his investigation at the residence, and he, himself would contact the Bishop personally. How odd he thought that a nun would be outside the Convent, let alone in the condition described by the police officers, for it was an unbending Convent rule that no nun was allowed to leave, except for the abbess.

Luis and the Bishop had been classmates so it was not difficult for Luis to get an appointment to see him. At the meeting, the condition of confidentiality was again imposed, to be effective until such time as a decision was made to make the information public. Luis commented that there were several foreign media people in Chucaya, as well as from other parts of Zambilla, was their presence connected to the nun story? The Bishop suspected it was for there had been several requests to interview him, none of which have been granted.

"The nun was from the Convent. She said she ran away because of what she claimed was the unbearable situation that existed there. The Convent had been taken over by a demonic force and many of the sisters had been possessed by the Devil and were behaving in a frightening way. The Bishop emphasized that these were the words the nun used. He ordered an immediate investigation. In answer to Luis' question as to how the nun described what she meant when she said the sisters were behaving in a frightening way, the Bishop said he was not able to reveal that."

"Luis, did those telephone calls last night have to do with this situation?" asked Marisa. He said they did and that what he had just said was all he knew.

Upon leaving the restaurant Alice asked whether the Convent was still on their afternoon program. Ted felt it may not be the best time to go there, it sounded kind of risky. Marisa said if Alice and Ted wanted to take a ride there she had no problem in taking them, and that as a matter of fact it might be interesting to see if anything unusual was happening, at least on the outside. She doubted they would be allowed to enter based on what Luis had told them. Agreed, they would drive there.

*   *   *   *

On route to the Convent there wasn't much conversation. The three were musing over what they had heard from Luis. Once they reached the outskirts of Chucaya, an area of humble houses along unpaved roads, their road began a soft descent as it wound away from the base of the Sierra.

A scattering of hillocks, wooded areas, open savannah vistas suddenly vanishing behind another wooded area paraded outside the car windows. As they rounded a curb there in the distance as if sitting in the center of the road stood the Convent. The scene reminded Alice of the Yellow Brick Road of the Wizard of Oz with the castle sitting at the far end.

"What an ideal setting for a religious retreat," commented Ted.

"Lovely," added Alice, "it's so quiet and peaceful out here, idyllic I would say. How could one be closer to God than at that place, and yet so…" hesitating for a moment as if a qualifying thought had arisen, "and yet, so vulnerable I guess is the word I'm looking for."

Nature has been kind to us in this small corner of the world," said Marisa. "I'm going to stop for a moment to show you an example." She directed their attention to a clump of trees with odd shaped leaves. "Notice how the leaves resemble human lungs. People around here use them to treat tuberculoses, pneumonia and other lung ailments, and swear by their effectiveness. Zambilla has many more of these products of nature which have marvelous health benefits."

Alice got out of the car and snipped off a couple of the leaves. Marisa said they could come back to this area if Alice and Ted wished, but it was time to continue on before it got dark.

As they drew nearer to the Convent, it was obvious it wasn't in the center of the road, for the road had dipped and curved to the right as it approached and then passed the Convent some fifty yards from its north wall.

There were two police vehicles and two unmarked black sedans in front of the Convent gate. Marisa turned into the driveway. As she did, two police officers and two civilians got out of their vehicles. No, it would not be possible to enter the Convent. Marisa asked why the police were there.

"Can't answer that question," said an officer and suggested they move on.

"Whose cars are these," asked Marisa pointing to the sedans, "looks like whoever came in them were allowed to enter."

A second officer motioned energetically with his arms for them to leave, "the Convent is closed to all visitors, now leave."

On their way back to Chucaya Alice asked if the others noticed how quiet it was around the Convent. Marisa said the civilians spoke Spanish with an Italian accent.

*   *   *   *

Over the next two days the Bishop's residence was a beehive of activity. Unable to get through to the Convent by phone, the Bishop instructed the pastor of the Saint Anthony Church to find out what has happened and to report back to him. Father Manfredo would have been the logical person to go to the Convent but he was in Santa Fé, so the pastor decided to go there with the Convent's regular woman doctor. Unable to convince the nuns to allow him to enter or to speak to the abbess, the pastor did succeed in having the doctor allowed in.

In her report, the doctor said she found nothing abnormal in the nuns she examined, at least with respect to vital signs and general health condition, however, she found the behavior of some of them alarming. These were not the same nuns she had known over the years. She recommended a psychiatrist examine them.

Across the ocean in the Vatican, a meeting was held in the office of the Prefect of the Congregation for Divine Worship and the Discipline of the Sacraments to discuss the flow of disturbing information from Chucaya. Aware of the huge problems facing the Church as a consequence of pedophile accusations against its priests in the United States, it was decided the Vatican would conduct direct and immediate investigations of the Zambillan situation. To this end, it would send four people to Chucaya, three priest exorcists and a priest psychiatrist.

When the four Vatican representatives departed from Rome for Zambilla, they were spotted by an Italian reporter who, after a little sleuthing around, obtained their names and destination, as well as their duties in the Vatican. Word circulated around Europe, which explains why a number of foreign media people were now in Chucaya.

CHAPTER 5

▼

Unable to sleep, Alice quietly put her bathrobe on in the dark, went down to the kitchen and poured herself a glass of milk. On her way back to her room, she was startled momentarily as she ran into Luis. She told him about her sleep problem. He said what worked for him was to turn on his night table light and read for a while. He suggested she give it a try, but since she couldn't do it without disturbing Ted, why not go into Luis' library. There she could pick out a book and relax in the alpaca chair.

Feeling embarrassed at being found walking around in the middle of the night, she figured it would only be civil to follow his suggestion. He accompanied her to the library, turned on the lights and wished her a good rest of the evening. Alice wondered what he was doing walking around at that hour of the night.

The bookshelves covered two complete walls with volumes on a wide variety of subjects. How to make a selection. Best pick out a thin book, and since she was a rapid reader perhaps she could finish it that evening. After a brief search, she found *The Ultimate Savage*, a short, fifty-page book and, thankfully, in English. The introduction told Alice the following pages were about the slaughter of Incas and the plunder of their riches by the Spanish Conquistador Francisco Pizarro. Alice sat back in Luis' comfortable chair and began reading. The more she read, the more engrossed she became, all the way to page 50. What savagery, what a blight on human history she thought as she placed the book back on the shelf. She would tell Ted about it the next day.

Perhaps the blame could be placed on her choice of reading material but Luis' remedy for sleeplessness failed to produce an immediate result as Alice lay in bed looking into the darkness of the room and thinking about the carnage committed by the Spaniards. Gradually, the defining borders of her mental images faded away and everything turned into a slow-moving mist and she a spirit floating through time, all the way back to the 15th Century. Slowly, the mist differentiated into recognizable shapes; she saw Spaniards in full armor mounted on huge stallions, behind them hundreds of foot soldiers led by the splendidly dressed commander whom she instinctively knew was Francisco Pizarro the Conquistador.

Alice turned anxious. A strange, unfamiliar force pulled her reluctant gaze to a nearby field where she saw thousands of Inca warriors and standing in their midst the Emperor. Prescience warned Alice she was witnessing the setting for an imminent catastrophe. She struggled to get away but the force immobilized her. She tried to blot out the scene by closing her eyes but succeeded only in opening them even wider.

Borne on a litter, the Inca Emperor entered a courtyard followed by his soldiers. Standing in its center was Pizarro and a priest. Hidden behind the walls of the surrounding buildings, Alice saw the armored horsemen mounted on their stallions and foot soldiers lying in wait like tightly wound coils ready to spring.

"Go back, go back," struggled Alice to warn the Emperor but her voice was only thoughts.

The priest approached the Emperor and addressed him. "I am the bearer of Christian faith," and handed him the Bible. Alice tried to run to the Emperor to warn him, but she had no legs. The Emperor took the Bible, looked at it and then threw it to the ground.

"No! No!" screamed Alice.

The echo of the Bible hitting the ground hurt Alice's ears as it reverberated loudly around the courtyard. The priest ran to Pizarro shouting, "God, God." The horsemen and foot soldiers burst into the courtyard and began cutting down the frightened Incas. It was only when the darkness of night made it impossible to find more escaping Incas did the carnage cease.

Alice's tears fell over the thousands and thousands of blood soaked bodies covering the landscape and became a river of red that slowly washed the bodies away.

Over the sound of her agony, Alice heard the voice of the Conquistador say to the captured Emperor that he would be allowed to go free if he filled the room with gold and silver. She saw a multitude of native Indians from all parts of the Kingdom converging on a room where they deposited sumptuous golden and silver pieces until the room was filled to the ceiling. In another room, the Emperor, shorn of his royal vestments, stood before Pizarro with a crucifix in his hands. He had converted to Christianity.

The greater and more desperate were Alice's efforts to reach the Emperor to snatch him away, the further he receded from her until from a far distance she saw soldiers place an iron collar around the Emperor's neck and tighten it until his head fell to the ground. The scene misted away before Alice's eyes, only the cries of anguish remained.

"Alice, Alice wake up," said the voice of Ted Shaw as he gently shook her shoulders.

CHAPTER 6

▼

The next morning, Alice hardly looked at her breakfast, her thoughts and talk were exclusively about last night's experience. What troubled her mostly was the feeling she had throughout the dream that what was happening to the Inca Emperor was her fault for not rescuing him, for she well knew the dangers that awaited him at each turn. It was as if she bore a cultural *mea culpa*, after all had not her information about the course of events come from a book, the product of her culture. The Incas had no books or writing.

Ted said people do have the strangest dreams and was about to describe one of his own when Marisa walked into the room. "Alice was telling me about a strange dream she had last night," informed Ted.

Acknowledging his comment with a half smile, Marisa said that apparently Luis had not told them what happened last night. Alice told Marisa she looked upset, and, no, Luis had not told them anything.

Last night an American news channel reported that demons had taken over a convent of nuns in Chucaya, Zambilla and that there were reports the Vatican was engaging in a cover-up. Within an hour the story was reported on a website devoted to mystical and paranormal phenomena. The media across the world seemed to have picked up on the story, including national television. Word of this was speeding across Chucaya and other Zambillan cities.

A maid who was serving more coffee told Marisa that Luis was up practically the whole night either watching television, on his computer or making telephone calls. Alice recalled running into him. Why hadn't he told her anything about this she wondered. A second maid entered the room saying there was a call for Señor Ted from Señor Pradilla.

After talking with Luis for a few minutes, Ted returned to the breakfast table and said that Luis wanted to make sure they had been informed of what happened last night. He suggested they stay put until there was a clearer picture of what the aftermath of last night's revelation will be. His people in Santa Fe reported an increasing number of foreign media people were arriving there on their way to Chucaya. The road to the Convent has been closed to all but official vehicles.

Marisa excused herself to attend to some business saying she should be back in a couple of hours.

Ted and Alice watched television. Half-understood newscasts all but pre-empted the local channels. There were archive shots of the Convent and the Vatican, there was a live scene of the roadblock, as well as interviews with clergymen and laymen, including one with the Mayor of Chucaya. Playing with the television controls Ted stumbled onto a channel from the States. Sandwiched between the latest sports and weather reports was a 15-second reference to the Convent situation. It added nothing to what Ted and Alice already knew.

Enough of looking at the screen, it was a cool, sunny morning, what better time to go for a walk and fresh air. Alice went to the kitchen to let the maids know they were going out. She saw both of them on their knees before a candle, reciting prayers. She closed the door noiselessly. When she told Ted about this he said perhaps they should give serious thought to leaving Zambilla, as Luis in his diplomatic way seemed to be suggesting they do. Alice was closed to any such idea.

They had walked no more than 10 minutes when Marisa's car pulled into the driveway. She motioned for them to come to her. Events had taken a disturbing twist. Without further explanation, she took both by their arms and led them into the house and out to the veranda.

Two lay women in the town were behaving like the possessed Convent nuns. What exactly took place was not reported, but both women had been rushed to the hospital for observation. City officials were privately concerned that this may be a prelude to something even bigger. Ted suggested they turn on the TV, perhaps they could get more details about this. Why not call Luis suggested Alice.

"No, I don't think we should bother him right now, I'm sure he is tied up with what's happening. He'll call us when he is able to," countered Marisa.

TV news cameras were focused on the hospital where the two women had been taken. According to the hospital spokesman, the women were responding favorably to medications and were resting quietly. When they arrived at the hospital they were in a heightened state of anxiety. It was learned that neither woman was epileptic nor were there any family histories of epilepsy. When a reporter asked whether they were possessed, the spokesman ended the news conference by walking away.

"That was an idiotic mistake," shouted Marisa, "he should have said something, anything to calm tensions instead of just walking off like that. It is only going to give rise to all kinds of dark interpretations. The media will feast on that."

A maid entered the room holding a telephone, it was Señor Pradilla for Señorita Marisa. After inquiring about the Americans' decision on staying or leaving, Luis said that two conferences were to be held at the Bishop's residence that very evening, arranged by the Vatican's chief representative who had recently arrived in Chucaya. The purpose of the first conference was to provide a full report on what has happened to date, both as to the Church's activities as well as those of the civil authorities. The second conference would be conducted by three clergy professionals from the Vatican to speak on the subject of demonic possession. Luis was unable to arrange for Marisa or Ted or Alice to attend but promised to report on what occurred once he returned home.

During the time elapsed between this telephone conversation and the beginning of the conference at the Bishop's residence, ripple effects from the TV disclosure on the Convent were in rampant motion. In an effort to circumvent the police roadblock, a plucky foreign journalist and his cameraman tried to get to the Convent by going through the surrounding woods. They were spotted and later expelled from the country.

Hoping to catch the nuns in compromising positions, a well-known publisher of pornographic magazines rented a helicopter and had it hover over the Convent with a slew of high-powered cameras focused on different areas of the grounds. A police helicopter forced the airborne voyeurs back to Chucaya.

In the city itself, people were descending on churches and tying up the telephone lines to the different parishes, in both cases beseeching priests with questions about the dangers posed by the happenings of the Convent now that two lay women had been possessed. "What can we do to ward off the demons," was the repeated questions hurled at the clergymen.

After dinner Ted and Alice again turned to the TV for the latest news. They discovered that if what was to transpire within the walls of the Bishop's residence was strictly confidential, the fact that the meeting was taking place was not. The street in front of the residence was crowded with reporters and cameramen plus an increasing number of curious onlookers. When the first conference attendees had difficulty in getting past the crowd, those who followed were conducted into the residence through a back entrance.

"Telephone for Señora Alice" said the maid, "it is Señorita Marisa."

"There has been a last minute no-show at the Bishop's conference and Luis has managed to get me in, informed Marisa, "I'll let you know what happens."

✳   ✳   ✳   ✳

Inside the Bishop's residence the invitees were assembled in the library where folding chairs had been set out in a semi-circular configuration. The group was animated in low-voiced conversations. Luis was talking to the President of the Zambilla Red Cross when he spotted Marisa entering the room. He waived to her.

A look around the room convinced Marisa that the most influential personages of Chucaya were assembled there. The chieftains of government, industry, commerce, law enforcement and even entertainment. The thought crossed her mind that should a bomb be dropped on the place it would blow away the heart of the city.

The Bishop's Secretary entered the room and asked the invitees to take their seats. He was followed by the Bishop and the Vatican's representative.

The Bishop opened the conference by indicating that it was the wish and conviction of the Church that with the collective cooperation and leadership of all the attendees, the serious problem of the Convent and its threatened metastasis into the city itself would not only be controlled but overcome. What people believe and act upon is heavily influenced by those who are viewed as community leaders, such as those present in that room.

The Vatican representative minced no words in declaring that what was occurring in the Convent was found by the Church to be cases of demonic possession. Medical and psychological tests left little doubt about this diagnosis. This straightforward declaration stirred up a buzz in the room. Instantly, arms waived for recognition. The Secretary reminded the invitees that they were to hold all questions for the end of the speaker's talk.

The speaker continued. The Church's conclusion as to the situation in the Convent did not necessarily apply to the cases of the two women who had recently been brought to the hospital allegedly showing symptoms generally associated with those that characterize possession cases. These women had not been examined by the Church since it had no jurisdiction over them, but it would be glad to do so if asked. However, it was to be noted in passing that it was not unusual in the wake of actual cases of demonic possession that persons with certain susceptibilities may react in a deceptively similar way. These cases must first be carefully diagnosed in order to rule out medical or psychiatric causes. Only then will the Church become involved, if requested.

It was essential that citizens occupying positions of influence in the community cooperate in helping maintain calm and good sense in order to prevent the spread of panic rumors. Working together, the Church and responsible civil leaders can put an end to the Convent situation with minimum harm to the community.

Marisa never was interested in the kind of public relations, social-unitedness kind of rallying she was hearing. What she wanted was to learn about the heart of the problem, so she decided to go to the conference being held in another room where the subject of demonic possession was to be discussed.

*   *   *   *

Neither thought they'd be watching so much TV during their stay in Zambilla, but here they were again switching from channel to channel with no fixed objective in mind, except to find one where Spanish was spoken at a speed that showed compassion for beginners.

Why don't we just talk a while said Ted as he turned off the set. They had not had much time to sit alone and calmly discuss what had happened since their arrival.

Ted missed being able to back off and analyze situations. Events had followed each other so rapid-fire-fast here that there never seemed to be time for quiet contemplation, very different from the situation he was accustomed to at his workplace where he breathed the air of careful consideration, calculation and analysis of risk factors and statistics.

Alice said she was pleased that both Luis and Marisa were keeping them informed on what was occurring. She was beginning to feel like a player—at least in a vicarious way—in the unfolding drama. This was definitely promising to be the most exciting vacation she had ever had, for which Ted was to be thanked, though she suspected he was beginning to regret having come up with the idea for this trip.

There was an urgent knocking at the front door followed by some excited, loud talking. Ted got up to look. Standing in the doorway was a tall, full-bearded young man who, when he saw Ted, pushed his way past the maid who had answered the door.

"Señor Americano, yes," he asked, and before Ted could answer he handed him an identification card. Ted called Alice.

The card had the man's picture on it, beard and all, and said, as far as the couple could tell, that he was a reporter for El Clarin newspaper. His name was Rafael Cortaza. Over the next five minutes there was a stumbling exchange of statements and questions conducted in short subject-verb sentences of slow Spanish garnished with occasional words in mispronounced English, at the end of which Ted and Alice concluded that what the reporter was probably saying was that there was a Convent nun who wanted to talk to someone in English. It was *urgente*, and *por favor* please go with him right now. He could not locate Luis.

Alice turned to the maid—who during the conversation had stood transfixed with her fingers covering her mouth as in frozen surprise—and asked if she knew this man and did he work for Luis' newspaper. The maid confirmed his identity. Ted wished Luis or Marisa were there. Did Alice and he really understand what was said? Alice thought they did. Then it occurred to her, how could they meet with a Convent nun if the road to the Convent was closed except for official vehicles. Rafael Cortaza explained that "*dee seester* house of *mi tio*.

His uncle's house, sounded safe enough to Alice. Let's go with him, we'll be able to actually talk to one of the nuns, how many non-Church people have been able to do that.

But Ted had reservations. Would they be doing something illegal? There were road blockades, quarantines, government involvement, and besides, this was a foreign country, the whole Convent thing was now front-page stuff. The bottom line spelled out risk. Perhaps they should wait for Luis. Alice would have none of this skittishness, moreover, the reporter said it was *muy urgente*, and he wasn't willing to wait for his boss. They wrote a note for Luis and left with Rafael Cortaza.

During the drive to the uncle's house, Alice extracted a few more facts from the reporter. The nun was from Canada and spoke *poco Español*. She and nine other nuns had been removed from the Convent for safety reasons. She was staying temporarily at the reporter's uncle's house. The uncle was the deacon of one of Chucaya's churches. People believed the Devil himself had come to their town and were very frightened. He said he had his own protection and pointed to rosary beads hanging from the rear-view mirror.

*   *   *   *

Marisa was happy to see that the conference had not yet started. There were still people arriving, though most of the seats had been claimed. She found one in the middle of the next to last row. On the dais the diocese spokesman was standing behind the lectern waiting for the audience to settle in their seats, behind him were three clergymen. Judging from the people she recognized around the room, Marisa noted how different they were from those at the first conference. There were a few professors from the local university, a popular psychiatrist who wrote a regular column for Luis' newspaper and at least three medical doctors. There were also foreigners present, some speaking what she thought sounded like German.

The spokesman introduced the three religious as high-ranking Church experts on para-normal phenomena. He underscored their presence at the conference as proof of the Church's determination to resolve the Convent matter and to do so with visibility. Marisa heard a whispered voice from her right say that the Church appeared to have learned a lesson from the recent clergy sex scandals in the United States.

The first speaker, Father Russell, was the tallest of the three, well over 6 feet. He was dressed in the traditional black pants and shirt and ever-present white color. He spoke in flawless Spanish, slowly and deliberately, creating the immediate impression of complete and easy command of his subject matter, "demonic possession." He had personally examined what he referred to as the "affected nuns" and had studied reports prepared by others. His diagnosis was that their extraordinarily aberrant behavior could not be reasonably explained on somatic, psychological or psychiatric grounds. At the request from the audience for specifics regarding the non-medical examinations, the speaker began to expound on the nature of the tests when, noticing a growing restlessness in the audience at the abstruseness of the explanation, the diocese spokesman suggested that all questions be held until after the speakers had finished their presentations.

Bringing his discourse back to easier to understand terms, Father Russell said the centuries of accumulated experience and information had allowed the Church to identify the genuine telling signs of demonic possession. What characterized these he summarized as being the total deviation from the person's normal behavior, knowledge or abilities accompanied by the powerful sensation that the victim had dropped the reins of control over his or her person with the accompanying sense that someone or something had taken over the body. Among the most frequently occurring signs were when the afflicted person begins to speak in a foreign or, at times, unknown language, accurately predicts future events, exhibits intense hatred for religious objects, has physical strength far beyond human capacity, contorts the body into impossible positions, utters foul and blasphemous language and emits noxious body odors.

A voice out of the audience asked whether any of the nuns were able to float. From several places in the room voices could be heard asking, "What did he say?"

The diocese spokesman was about to remind the questioner of the rule regarding audience questions when Father Russell said he would answer the question now. He new what the questioner was alluding to and he also knew that more often than not this and related questions were directed to him in a taunting spirit, referring as they did to ancient practices not limited to the Church and which, in any event, had long been abandoned.

During the period between 1400 and 1700 there was what could be considered near hysteria over the alleged existence of witches, sorcerers and demons that it was widely believed caused people to become possessed. Trials and executions for suspected practitioners of these nefarious occupations were widespread, particularly in Europe.

In order to determine whether a person was a witch or sorcerer or possessed, people allowed their imaginations to run rampant and as a result came up with an assortment of bizarre tests. One of these was the one alluded to by Father Russell's questioner, the so-called *floating test* whereby a suspect was held suspended by ropes over a body of water, often in a large tub-like receptacle. Gradually, he or she was lowered into the water and then released. If the person floated it was a sign he or she was actually possessed or was a witch or sorcerer, this being such a supra-natural feat that only someone with supernatural powers like those possessed by the Devil himself could accomplish it.

There were other tests applied, two of the most popular were the "tears" and the "marks" tests. The first consisted of having the suspect concentrate his or her attention on a holy image, often of Christ on the Cross, and then to graphically describe to the suspect the suffering endured by Christ. If this did not cause tears to flow, it had to be because the person was possessed or otherwise influenced by the Devil.

The other test was based on the belief that if a demon had entered a person's body, he must have left a mark of some kind at the point of entrance. To facilitate the search for the mark the person's clothing and all body hair including eyebrows were removed.

All of this Father Russell knew when he answered the questioner by simply saying the Church had progressed greatly since the times of the test alluded to and that today scientific methods were being employed.

*　　　*　　　*　　　*

The deacon was a chubby, cherub-looking person who one would think had no business wearing the look of apprehension he had on his face. As he led Ted, Alice and Rafael into his small office, he said he wasn't sure he was doing the right thing, for the good sister had been placed with him with the understanding, albeit tacit, that she would be his responsibility. But her request to speak to someone in English who was not a religious was made with such fervent sincerity and passion that he found himself incapable of refusing. She was upstairs and he would bring her down, but it must be remembered she had been through some awful experiences.

Alice wasn't sure what the deacon meant by his last statement, after all it was the nun who requested the meeting. One thing was for sure, Alice was sitting on the proverbial pins and needles. What's wrong with me, she thought, I'm acting like some nervous teenager waiting for her date to arrive.

"I'm sorry," said the deacon, "I neglected to ask your names, but this is Sister Teresa."

Her habit was gray with a pale white stripe bordering the hood-like headpiece; she smiled nervously as she extended her hand. She squeezed Alice's in a way that made Alice feel it was meant to communicate something. The deacon motioned for her to sit in a comfortable upholstered chair that she declined in favor of a plainer one. The nun reached inside her habit and pulled out rosary beads that she then held on her lap.

"Thank you for coming here this evening, it is so kind of you," began the nun.

"I understand you are Canadian, is that right, Sister Teresa."

"It is so good to hear English spoken and, yes, I am Canadian, from Toronto. I arrived here in Chucaya about a year ago, knowing very little Spanish. I requested to be sent here. The reason I asked this very good man—she nodded to the deacon—to find a lay person who understood English was to allow me to describe my recent experiences in the Convent free of any language barrier and to hopefully help relieve some of the anguish I have inside of me."

She hesitated a moment as if reconsidering what she was about to say. "I also want the truth to be known, and God forgive me for this, should the Church authorities be reluctant to reveal all." Convinced it would be better that he not hear any more of this, the deacon stood up and excused himself saying he would be in the next room should he be needed. As he walked out, the nun fixed her eyes on the rosary beads resting on her lap in what Alice interpreted as a gesture of painful resolve.

"Something evil is in the Convent," began the nun. "I fear it may soon spread throughout the city. It is powerful and depraved." She paused, the muscles around their mouth tried to tense but only quivered. Alice asked whether she preferred to rest a few moments, or perhaps she could get her something. Instead of answering, the nun went on to explain that it was about seven days ago that she first heard rumors that the abbess, Sister Dolores, was acting oddly. She had become increasingly more reclusive. From the moment the sun went down her rooms were in absolute darkness, where before they were often well lighted as she usually worked late. When she did emerge from her rooms she looked tired and haggard. Her personality too had abruptly changed. She was unnaturally mean and sharp-tongued, constantly reprimanding and scolding the nuns, only to abruptly turn sweet and mellifluous. Gradually, she limited her attendance at religious services and spiritual exercises. On one occasion, she jumped up from her bench in the chapel and rushed out unsteady on her feet. The nuns seated near the door said that her face was swollen out of shape.

Sister Teresa paused for a moment and closed her eyes as if in meditation. Her lips began to move but no sound came out. Not wanting to interfere with whatever was happening, the others in the room refrained from speaking or moving.

Acting exclusively on internal stimuli, the nun resumed speaking, this time without looking at anyone and appearing to be focusing on a scene in her mind. Her first direct experience occurred one evening a little after midnight. She had always been a light sleeper and usually awoke at the slightest noise. This particular night she heard a sound she couldn't identify, like a throaty voice. But she saw nothing unusual. The noise ceased.

The following evening, she was again awaked this time by several of the same identical sounds, but now coming from different areas of the dormitory. How can I describe these sounds, she thought. They will think I am unbalanced, but I must tell the truth of what I believe.

She said what she heard were deep masculine voices, though at times she felt it was a single voice coming simultaneously from different places. The voices seemed to be that of someone struggling against a resistance of some kind, as if trying to squeeze into or out of something. She sat up but could not see who or what was producing the sounds. As her eyes adjusted to the darkness, she saw that in some of the cots there were motions like the turning and twisting of bodies. She became frightened. The next morning no one mentioned anything, so she refrained from bringing it up. Perhaps it was all a dream.

However, two events the following day lent credence to the possible reality of the occurrences of the past two evenings. The first took place as the nuns were leaving the Convent church after morning mass. Sister Isabel, who was walking in front of her, suddenly turned and with a peculiar grin on her face said that Sister Teresa's mother, who was in a mental institution, had committed suicide. Sister Teresa swooned. The following day she was able to verify that what Sister Isabel had said was in fact true. What was bizarre was that the suicide had not yet occurred at the time Sister Isabel made the revelation.

The second event occurred during the afternoon. There was a commotion in the embroidery work place. Nuns were hurrying in that direction. On the floor twisting and writhing were sisters Jeanne and Magdalene, their bodies going into impossible convulsions and their faces hideously swollen. The nuns stood around watching in disbelief and frightened when the abbess pushed her way through the group until she stood directly over the convulsing sisters. She remained there for a few minutes and with unblinking eyes absorbed the scene before her. The two bodies ceased convulsing and lay motionless. She ordered the two sisters be taken to her rooms. Sister Teresa noticed that the abbess was not wearing the large crucifix that usually hung from her waist.

Following the incident in the embroidery room, things got unhinged. Nuns could be found in convulsions everywhere. Some began to howl like animals, their faces distorted. Some tore off their habits and said and did things too vulgar and revolting for her to repeat. At that point she looked as if she was about to faint. Ted and Rafael Cortaza rushed to steady her. She was taken to her room where the deacon's wife attended to her.

*   *   *   *

Back at the Bishop's residence, the next speaker was introduced, his subject was the history of demonic possession. These words reminded Marisa of the sharp contrasts in the room. Two of the religious on the dais with their long gray robes and sandals, huge crucifixes resting on their breasts, and thick cords hanging loosely from their waists, stirred up medieval images. In contrast, in the audience computer laptops were being fingered, recorders were busy spinning and camcorders were aiming at the speakers.

The speaker commenced with examples of demonic possession occurring among closely knit social units such as nuns in a convent setting. The most well-known and celebrated case was the one that occurred in the French town of Loudon during the mid-1630s involving a whole convent of Ursuline nuns. Then there were the cases of possessed nuns in Aix-en-Provence, Lille and Louviers, all in France.

With the purpose of establishing a biblical foundation for belief in demonic possession, the speaker reached back to the time of Jesus Christ and cited an example taken from the Gospel of Saint Mark. Coming from the Sea of Galilee Jesus entered the land of Gerasenes where he was met by a man "from tombs cut into the mountains." The man, it was claimed, possessed an unclean spirit. Nothing could bind him, not even chains. When he saw Christ approaching the man went to him seeking help. Christ summoned the demon spirit to leave the man and asked the spirit's name, "My name is Legion," answered the spirit "for we are many." Once the demons left the man, Jesus sent them into a nearby herd of swine, which then jumped into the sea and drowned.

Assuming the tone of the clinician, the speaker continued. Since the beginning of the beginning Satan has roamed the world in search for opportunities to implement his gospel of evil. In doing this, he does not work alone for, as he boasted to Christ, they are legion. Over the ages, the Church has assembled a list of his accomplices who have identified themselves, such as Asmodeus, Zabulon, Isacaaron, Gresil, Amand, Celsus, Cham and Ureil for example.

In accomplishing his possession, Satan or one of his accomplices infiltrates and then takes over the physical and mental faculties, but not the soul, of the victim. It is over the possession of the soul that Satan and the exorcist will battle. It was to be noted, he pointed out, that he had referred to the possessed person as the "victim" implying that he or she is blameless of what happens. In all of the recorded cases, it was found that the possession had occurred against the person's will. This is so even in those cases where the afflicted person has signed a pact with the Devil.

Noticing the looks of surprise and in many cases of incredulity in the audience, the speaker hastened to add that he appreciated the fact that modern ears find talk about people making a pact with the Devil as something pretty farfetched, or perhaps it brought to mind Goethe's *Faust*, the classical masterpiece on the subject of selling one's soul to the Devil, and that it had the ring of ignorant superstitions straight out of the Dark Ages. Yet, he added, there existed a whole body of evidence and history surrounding this phenomenon. Years ago documents written in blood which were alleged to be Pacts with the Devil were actually introduced in courts as evidence of demonic possession.

Sensing continued skepticism in the audience, the speaker followed his customary tactic and switched the topic to one that was closer to the Church's direct experience. He said no one is immune to demonic possession not even Saints such as Thomas Aquinas, Francis of Assisi, Catherine of Sienna, John of the

Cross, and, allegedly, also Sister Teresa of Calcutta who when it was feared she was being attacked by Satan was recently exorcised.

During intermission Marisa walked among the audience greeting a few acquaintances and listening to comments on what had been said thus far. She stopped to chat with a friend and two others when a fourth person joined the group and immediately posed a question.

"What I fail to understand and what makes this whole Church approach to this Convent thing sound so unreal is why the so called demons should wait some three or four hundred years before again invading—if that's the right word—a convent. What did they do during this period, go on sabbatical or what?"

Marisa's friend was visibly perturbed by the flippant manner in which the question was framed, and in a didactic manner—not difficult for him to adopt since he was a university professor—was quick to point out that if the premise is accepted that we are dealing with beings or forces which exist in a spiritual or non-material plane, then the element of time may be very different from that in which we live. For instance, what for us would be three or four hundred years may be an instant of time for them. And what if time as humans experience it does not exist at all on their plane so that everything that happens, happens in the present. The questioner shrugged his shoulders and walked away.

Marisa made her way over to another group engaged in lively conversation and listened.

"I have the feeling we're not being told the whole truth about what's happening in the Convent. Why are only certain people allowed to enter there, why the big mystery."

"What troubles me is that people outside the Convent, right here in Chucaya, have been affected or should I say possessed."

"Personally, I think this is all a bunch of nonsense, all this talk about demons and stuff. What is needed is a heavy hand against those nuns, whip the foolishness out of them is what I say."

"Wrong, wrong approach, absolutely wrong, what is needed is for the nuns to be given more freedom, more contact with the wider world. Being locked up the way they are would bring anyone's emotions to the boiling point. One small incident and bang, an explosion."

"You know, I did a little reading on this subject and I think the answer was found centuries ago. What the nuns are suffering from was even given a name and a very descriptive name at that, "Furor Uterinus," and I don't believe I have to translate that for you. Debarred from men, this is certainly a possibility. But forget about the Church accepting this."

"You are all missing the obvious, what is needed in this hedonistic world is a return to our basic moral values and a lot of praying to God."

Father Giovani was clearly the oldest of the religious on the dais; he was the Church's most experienced and learned exorcist. Over the past few years the number of exorcisms he was called upon to treat had fallen, but he was still the Church's Dean of Exorcists, an exaltation that carried with it the assignment to the more complex cases. Added to this were his duties as teacher and mentor to young exorcist priests. The combined weight of these duties was beginning to sap his physical and mental stamina, all of which rendered retirement ever more appealing. Perhaps not a full retirement. Something related to the seminary preparation for priesthood. The seminary in Bologna sounded good to him.

He knew his material well and had organized it so clearly and efficiently that he could deliver a lecture by simply turning on the playback of his mental recorder. Here he was in Chucaya, Zambilla on what he hoped would be his last exorcism. If he had not been asked to come here by high Vatican authorities, he would have sent a younger priest in his place.

As he waited his turn to speak his eyes swept over the audience. How he wished he could take these people beyond the mechanics of exorcism and into the scorching center of the battleground where the exorcist and the Satan encounter each other, spar, feint and finally lock themselves in a ferocious spiritual clash. But he knew this was not possible. How could he ever convey or give even an iota of a glimpse into the ineffable pain and anguish the exorcist endures in the struggle fought in a timeless, spaceless netherworld where the prodigious forces of Good and Evil vie for conquest and domination of the victim's soul.

The situation here in Chucaya was the worst he had ever experienced, equal, if not greater, to those that occurred back in the 17th Century which he often used as case studies in his exorcism classes back in Rome. Here the Evil had moved beyond a specific group and threatened to propagate out into the masses.

This demonic onslaught will call for superhuman spiritual strength, he mused. Was he up to it? Was there enough remaining in him to successfully undertake this mission? Would God give him the strength to succeed? He looked down at his folded hands and felt a foreboding chill of the Evil.

After a short introduction of credentials, Father Giovanni stepped up to the lectern. He was the most striking figure of the three speakers. Aside from his monk-like habit there was his complete baldness, long, white beard and a hood that rested on his shoulders. The look in his eyes seemed to come from deep recesses, as if they were apertures through which his thoughts and emotions were directly exposed.

Marisa was so taken up with the appearance of the speaker she had not noticed that the chairs to her right and to her left were now occupied by new people. The one to her right, who later introduced himself as a reporter for a national maga-zine, was busy setting up his laptop. On her left was a rotund mass of flesh that over-occupied his chair and whose name she instantly realized she was not inter-ested in knowing. He had the annoying habit of constantly clearing his throat of something or other. After each particularly loud clearing effort, he would turn to anyone whose attention he may have attracted and flash an absurd grin. The louder the noise the broader the grin, as if it were registering the decibel level.

As the speaker progressed through his talk, Marisa's attention was attracted to her neighbor's laptop. A slight tilting of her head allowed her to read what he was writing. She soon realized what he was doing was capsulizing the speaker's state-ments and doing it amazingly fast and accurately. He flashed a smile at her and continued writing:

There are a diminishing number of exorcists today.

Priest's manual contains only exorcism rite approved by Church, called *Rituale Romanun* written 1614, amended slightly 1998.

(Marisa realized the laptop was sending information to some place, maybe to the guy's office.)

Before exorcism, priest must make good confession and be absolved so Satan not use them against him in exorcism.

Priest wears Alb, purple stole, ends placed on victim's neck.

Priest places right hand on head of victim—Jesus used hands to heal the sick.

Bible with old and new testaments always nearby.

This is like watching a foreign movie with a running translation at the bottom of the screen, thought Marisa as she bifurcated her attention between what the speaker was saying and the laptop summary. She continued reading:

Crucifix always present. Satan and evil spirits always look away from cross.

Exorcist alert against tricks, deceits of evil spirits who answer questions falsely try to confuse exorcist.

Evil spirits manifest themselves under pressure, hope exorcist will tire, leave them alone, will hide so exorcist believes they left body, makes victim pretend he's free of evil spirit.

Try get evil spirits give their names and say what keeping them in the victim— magical spell, sorcerer's symbol, occult document, etc…If victim swallowed any of these most vomit them up.

Exorcist risk of being overwhelmed by evil spirit and himself being possessed.

Marisa felt a tap on her shoulder, a young lady behind her pointed to the door where Luis was standing. He motioned her over. Outside in the corridor Luis told Marisa he had just learned that four more women had been taken to a hospital showing the same symptoms as the nuns. The authorities had decided to quarantine Chucaya from the rest of the country.

"What do you mean by quarantine? How can an entire city be quarantined," asked Marisa.

"The highways will be closed as well as air traffic in and out of Chucaya."

"But that sounds irrational, it will only exacerbate the situation in the city. When does all of this go into effect, do you know?"

No definite date has been announced but it was believed it would happen within the next 48 hours or so. He apologized for taking Marisa out from the conference but wanted to share this fresh news with her. What did she think they should tell Ted and Alice? Should they urge them to leave? He was pretty sure he could get them seats on a commercial flight out of here the next day.

No apology called for, she had heard enough about the exorcism for a while. As to Ted and Alice, of course they should be told about the quarantine. But it was really up to them to decide on what to do. From what she had seen so far, she could predict their individual reactions.

*   *   *   *

When, after returning with Ted and Alice from the meeting with the nun, Rafael Cortaza's car pulled into Luis' driveway, Luis' car was parked in front of the house. Luis heard Rafael's car drive up and came out of the house. With obvious nervousness Rafael explained what had happened. Luis told him he did the right thing in taking Ted and Alice to meet with Sister Teresa and that he should have a report on Luis' desk tomorrow. Relieved, Rafael drove away.

The remainder of the evening was devoted to exchanging reports on what had transpired. Luis mentioned the government's quarantine decision and said that he could arrange to get seats for Ted and Alice on one of the next day's flights to Santa Fe if they wished to leave. Beyond the next day, there were no assurances.

Ted said the idea of a quarantine was absurd almost ludicrous, what possible good would it accomplish, one might think the city was facing the Black Plague or some kind of bacterial or virus pandemic.

Alice did not hesitate to make her position clear, she had no intention of leaving. She wanted to see how this whole thing played out. Marisa smiled at Luis.

Ted was caught off balance by Alice's unilateral, no-discussion decision. There was momentary silence in the room, a silence waiting to be filled by Ted's response. Alice was about to speak when Ted finally spoke up.

"I'm sure you have all noticed that, well at least as far as I've been told, only women have been affected so far. Am I right?" Since no one indicated he was wrong, he continued. "That being so, and since Alice has elected to stay, how could I even begin to consider leaving."

If Ted had now answered the question of whether to go or to leave, he had replaced it with the uncertainty of whether his decision was based on the belief that his staying entailed no risk to him, or whether it indicated a *noblesse oblige* concern for Alice, or both.

Alice would have preferred that he share in at least a bit of the excitement she felt about what was happening. For reasons not entirely clear even to her, but in some way vaguely related to Ted's disappointing attitude, Alice spoke up saying what was unfolding in Chucaya was a once-in-a-lifetime human drama which she wouldn't miss for anything in the world. More than that, she yearned to get involved in some direct way. Turning to Luis she asked whether he thought there was a chance she might be able to. What did she have in mind? She had no precise idea on how to do so, she only wished there was a way for her to help solve the mystery of what was happening.

Luis reminded her she was a foreigner in the country and should be careful of what she did. Ted raised his eyebrows and sent an I-told-you-so look at Alice.

"By the way, with all that's been happening I forgot to mention something which should be of interest to all of you," exclaimed Luis as he snapped his fingers. At the Bishop's place he ran into Moss Hoover, an American who has lived in Zambilla for many years. Marisa knew him. He used to be a foreman of an American construction company that operated in the country. When he retired from the company he liked Zambilla so much that he decided to remain here. He is quite a colorful character, a pragmatic, outspoken, hard drinking, poker playing, earthy kind of person. He knows everyone and about everything that happens in this country. Luis told him about the American guests staying with him and mentioned the reason for their coming here, the blue people thing.

Moss knew a great deal about this Mr. Charlie person. He said Charles Theoros first came to Zambilla as commercial attaché to the Greek Embassy in Santa Fé. Seeing an opportunity to make money by exporting exotic animals from the Zambillan rainforest, he resigned and moved to the rainforest border town of Lepticia. Over the years the business grew, as did his problems with alcohol and his notoriously bad temper. It wasn't long before he became the central figure in Lepticia, feared for the ferocity of his temper outbursts, respected for the local employment his business produced, and admired for his ability to tread a narrow line between the legitimate and that which carried a jail sentence.

According to Moss, Charlie is no longer to be found in Lepticia having left in a hurry just as the authorities were about to descend upon him. It seems he had brought a young boy around 10 years old to Lepticia who he claimed came from high in the Sierra, a member of a nearly extinct tribe. The boy, who he called *Calamus,* spoke a language no one understood. Charlie said the boy could turn his body blue and that he, Charlie, planned to soon put him on exhibition.

But his efforts to get the boy to change color failed. He went so far as to paint first one then three of his young employees blue in the hope the Indian would get the idea and turn himself blue. Charlie became the butt of jokes, a new one every day it seemed.

One evening in a drunken rage he beat the Indian boy to death while repeating over and over again that he had spent a lot of money and time preparing for his big exhibition and the stupid, Indian bastard would pay for it.

"Oh my God, that's sick," exclaimed Alice.

"Of course you're right Alice," observed Marisa, but think for a moment. If Mr. Charlie went to all that trouble of bringing the boy down from the Sierra, doesn't that mean that he really must have seen blue people. Otherwise, why go through all that?"

"Good point," said Luis, "it never occurred to me."

CHAPTER 7

▼

It was not that he was generally opposed to Fidel Castro's iron-fisted rule over Cuba or to the Grand Jefe's Human Rights violations, for he was basically apolitical. His sole and consuming interest was in making money, something that had become virtually impossible to do in Cuba. He had been a wheeler-dealer extraordinaire until slammed down by Castro's goon squads and ended up being sent to prison for two years. The court's decision said he was found guilty of "Acts Undermining the Socialist Economy."

The thought of going to Miami had not even flickered across his mind, but on a Saturday morning in May of 1981, Germán García was taken from his prison cell to the seaport town of Mariel where he was put aboard an overly-crowded boat and dispatched to Miami along with 88,817 others whom Fidel Castro had released from jails and mental institutions.

After a brief period of acclimation in Miami, his keen scent for money-making opportunities combined with his glib salesmanship led him to his first business venture, which he financed with loans from fellow exiled relatives and recently made friends. From a rented storefront in Little Havana's Calle Ocho, he received food and medicine packages from local residents for delivery to families and relatives in Cuba. Once competition for these services heated up, he sold the business and went on to other ventures.

On this particular day Germán García, now the manager/owner of the Clothes-R-U Company, was busy making phone calls and firing off e-mails to Chucaya, Zambilla.

"I know, I know, there's no way for people to get into Chucaya by plane or by land, but listen, I can get you 5,000 T-shirts by tomorrow noon. I don't believe the travel ban covers cargo. Anyhow, I've checked and there is no ban on planes flying over the city, if necessary we'll airdrop the bundles damn it. Don't worry, you'll be informed of when and where. Just wire the money to my bank, you have the account number. Yes, yes, the shirts will have a large crucifix painted on both the front and the back. Remember, we can also send you all the rosary beads or anything else you want, even pictures of Saints with prayers in Spanish. I'll send you some samples."

At supermarkets, drug and convenience stores across America bundles of the latest edition of the tabloid "Galaxy" were being dropped off for placement next to checkout counters. The lead headline read, "Devil Invades the World" and below it a sketch of a diabolic figure hovering over Zambilla with outstretched arms covering the world. According to the cover story, after centuries of waiting and planning, Satan has dispatched his legions of evil spirits to the four corners of the world. Their first appearance has been made in Chucaya, Zambilla.

In the New York offices of the Randolf Publishing Company, Paul Schaffer, chief of the new books department, was pacing the floor and dressing down two of his associates.

"Find me someone, anyone in Zambilla who has any degree of direct knowledge about the Convent matter. We need a book out on this, and we need it fast. A few facts will be enough, we'll fill in the rest of the story. As soon as the book hits the stores and the Internet, we will have locked in the rights to a movie, not to mention HBO and other media outlets. But we've got to be first, not second, first, get it! The budget for this is generous so go out there and find me an author."

A late night infomercial from the U.S. offered a CD said to contain the voice of Satan himself recorded during Catholic, Islamic and Protestant Evangelical exorcisms. The CD was not for everyone, for the voice was so evil and macabre that people had been known to faint upon hearing it. Listeners were asked to dial 800-DEMONIC and have their credit cards ready. Price $29.95 for each CD and $9.95 for each cassette.

"Why not give it a shot," enthused Larry Bickford, Vice President of World-wide Travel Adventures, to his luncheon companion and company president Peter Drouple. "This whole Satan or Devil or whatever thing has caught the attention of millions," continued Bickford as his colleague savored his cup of sugared strawberries immersed in red wine. "Imagine the lure of the chance to fly over the Convent where supposedly the Devil himself is supposed to be."

Lowering the tone of his voice as he leaned towards Drouple, he whispered that maybe they can have someone say he or she felt vibrations like waves coming from the Convent. They could charge a healthy price for this. All that had to be done was to get permission to fly over the place and circle around it a few times. If necessary they could offer someone a percentage.

"We already know how to do business in those countries, don't we? Just deposit a let's call it an incentive fee, into a numbered account. Peter, I tell you we can make a few bucks on this."

*   *   *   *

In Chucaya the lines in front of churches—that earlier had been disorganized groups of people which priests, under the threat of otherwise closing the church doors, managed to reshape into more or less orderly lines—were long and growing. Luis stopped his car in front of one of them to inquire, and was told these were confession lines.

"Hearts free of sin are the best protection against demonic possession, confess your sins," shouted a woman standing in line.

"We need more priests," shouted another.

Arriving at his office, Luis tried unsuccessfully to contact the Bishop. He left a message. A few moments later the Bishop's secretary called to explain that the Bishop was at an important meeting with the pastors of the city's churches and an emissary from the Vatican. Told about what Luis had seen on his way to his office, the secretary breathed a nervous sigh of concern and said the situation was becoming worrisome. Priests were hearing confessions at 12-hours stretches and sometimes longer. To help alleviate the load priests were being brought in from other cities and towns from across the country. What was exacerbating their plight was the fact that people were going from priest to priest and from church to church making multiple confessions. Some said they had sinned since they confessed themselves a few hours earlier and needed to confess again. Attempts to convince people that multiple confessions were absolutely unnecessary had either fallen on un-listening ears or, in some instances, provoked angry remonstrations.

The Bishop had scheduled a televised address to the people in which he will explain in simple terms how confessions should be made and would implore viewers to please adhere to these rules. No decision had been made as to whether to tell viewers that confessions made in violation of the rules would be invalid, useless, and, worse, a sin. Luis agreed to publish something about this in the front page of the next edition and have one of his editors work with the secretary on the wording.

"Incidentally, and I tell you this off the record," added the secretary, "to give you an idea of how bad the situation had become, the Mayor and two councilmen in a meeting with the Bishop suggested he might wish to consider having group confessions performed. The idea was to have each person state his sins in a low voice to God himself at the end of which the priest would grant God's *en masse* absolution to the group and hand out the same penance for all. The Bishop, who, as you know is a kindly, warm, soft-spoken servant of our Lord, became upset. His voice cracked as he rejected what he called a blasphemy against the Church and one of its most important sacraments. Sternly, he told the government representatives to banish from their thoughts any possibility that the Church will sacrifice its holy institutions for the sake of helping the civil authorities carry out their official duties of maintaining civil order."

*   *   *   *

Ted watched Alice as she stepped out of the shower and again marveled at how beautifully proportioned her body was, every part sculptured to perfection. Youthful vitality, soft pink whiteness, abundant chestnut hair dancing in the wind of her hairdryer.

He was pleased and content. Why couldn't this be all there was. Why did there have to be doubts and uncertainties between them. He could not close his eyes to the obvious fact that they differed in the way they looked at the world and their places in it. At times, he wished he could be more like her, but too many years had hardened and encrusted his attitudes.

The dynamics of their relationship had changed. At the start, it was he who suggested things to do, which were the things that people did in his world. She followed apparently happily for this was a new experience for her, and he knew that fresh experiences were what fired her enthusiasm. But now the novelty had worn off and familiarity had set in and with it a teasing playfulness on her part about things that interested him and a revival of her thirst for new experiences, this time for those outside of Ted's world.

Being here in Zambilla at this time held out the promise of what she longed for. Ted wondered whether their relationship could survive being overwhelmed by events. Already, there were signs of the stress resulting from things like Alice's making solo decisions, decisions he would not have made.

Here in their borrowed room, Alice was again playing with his emotions as she walked towards him wrapped in a towel, eyes fixed on him, singing a sultry melody as her body moved with the seductiveness of an experienced temptress. Of course sex had been a huge part of it all. She had revitalized him, turned him into a man with the virility of someone half his age, though he was not convinced sex gave her that much pleasure, at least not with him. But she knew very well what it meant to him. Here she was again toying with him.

Standing inches from where he sat at the edge of the bed, she turned her head to the side so he could see the profile of her face, something she knew turned him on. Slowly she let the towel drop to the floor, and with theatrical motions kicked it across the room, like some unwanted, unneeded object.

Lying next to each other and existing somewhere in that melatonin place that separates wakefulness from deep sleep, the couple gradually returned to Chucaya, to Luis Carlos' house, to the bedroom, a fallen towel, and to a gentle knocking at the door and the apologetic voice of the maid. "Señora Alice, Señorita Marisa has arrived."

Marisa was standing in the patio conversing with Rafael Cortaza.

"Let me see if I understand," said, Marisa. "The nun that is staying at your uncle's house has asked you to deliver a note to Señorita Alice, and your uncle does not to know about this, is that right?"

"That's what I think she told me, her Spanish is not very good, but this is what I understood. She has put me in a terrible position. I wanted to help her but I didn't want to do anything behind my uncle's back."

"Did she give you the note and did you accept it?"

"Yes I did, but without really thinking."

"Well it seems to me that since you have taken the note you have an obligation to deliver it. Don't you agree? Do you have any idea what this is all about? Did the nun say anything else to you?"

"No, she only said deliver this to the American lady. She put the note in my hand and walked away."

"Had your uncle indicated anything unusual had happened?"

"No, only that the nun was very nervous."

"Do you have the note with you?"

He pulled a folded piece of yellow paper from the inside pocket of his jacket and held it out to her.

"No, don't give it to me, give it to the Señorita Alice when she comes down."

As they were going down the stairs Ted, rubbing his stomach, said he was famished and needed to replenish some of the energy he used up last night. "I'll tell the maid about your desperate state," smiled Alice. "As for me, I could have used a bit more sleep."

"This is the note," said Cortaza as he handed the wrinkled, folded sheet to Alice. She unfolded it and read. This is strange, what could have happened she wondered. Turning to Rafael she asked whether the nun was all right.

"For heaven's sake Alice, what does it say," implored Ted.

"I'll read it to you."

> *Mrs. Shaw, I've reached a breaking point. I must leave immediately, please come with a car to the deacon's house between 11 and 12 this morning. Stop directly in front of the front door. Timing is crucial, I pray you do not fail me.*
>
> *Blessings,*
> *Sister Teresa.*

The three looked at each other as if searching for an explanation. "Sounds serious," observed Ted, "if you'll remember, Alice, she looked awfully nervous last night."

"Can it have to do with the Convent possessions," asked Alice, "that would really be scary stuff wouldn't it?"

"Can't we just have Rafael go to the house, apparently what she wants is a ride," suggested Ted.

"That won't do," observed Marisa, "the request is directed to Alice and in any event if what she wanted was transportation she had Rafael right there."

"I'll go with Alice," offered Marisa, "you are going aren't you Alice?"

"Of course I am"

Ted, who by now had forgotten about his breakfast needs, wore an expression which announced to the world that he took a dim view of what had been decided. Turning to Alice he reminded her that he had made arrangements with his office to confer with people there to discuss important pending business matters so he would not be able to go with her. But in the future he intended to accompany her in all of her expeditions. He definitely wanted Rafael to accompany them on this one.

*   *   *   *

Unable to find any paper to write on Sister Teresa tore out the blank last page of her bible and with the stub of a pencil borrowed from the maid wrote:

Dear Deacon Botero,

I can no longer bear the agony I feel and I must leave. You and Mrs. Botero have been so kind and compassionate for which the Lord will surely bless you. Pray for me as I shall pray for both of you.

Blessings
Sister Teresa

She placed the note on the pillow of her bed, closed her suitcase, walked downstairs and sat in front of the window facing the driveway. It was not 11 o'clock. If the deacon and his wife stuck to their daily weekday practice, they would not return from the church until noontime. She prayed a Hail Mary that Alice had received her note and would be there soon.

Her mind was settled, she was leaving the country and returning to Canada. She was also leaving the religious life. No, she had not lost her faith but neither could she any longer carry on with her duties as a nun. What she had seen in the Convent had impressed her so profoundly that she was convinced she would be permanently affected. She didn't feel any sign of being possessed, yet, she had a constant sensation of being surrounded by a menacing evil.

Drifting in these thoughts, she failed to see Marisa's car coming up the driveway. Only when it stopped in front of her window did she notice. She embraced the maid, handed her a picture of the Virgin Mary with a short prayer, picked up her suitcase and walked out.

Alice introduced Marisa and the nun to each other. Then the inevitable question of where the nun wanted to go.

"I don't know, it will depend on what you kind ladies tell me," came the surprising response, "I will explain but please let us drive away from here, the deacon should be arriving soon."

Marisa suggested they drive a few blocks north to a restaurant on the left side of the street which had been closed for violation of regulations of some kind. They could park there for a while and talk.

As they drove into the parking lot, they saw a large sign posted on the restaurant door notifying the public that it was closed by order of the Chucaya Health Department and that anyone interested in this matter could obtain information at the Health Department's Restaurant Licenses Division. A yellow ribbon was stretched across the door telling the world not to pass. They noticed that all the windows had been broken.

Sister Teresa apologized for the hush, hush surrounding her note and proceeded to explain. She, as well as the other sisters who were removed from the Convent, had become a migraine for everyone. They were recluses, unable to leave the places where they were assigned. If they ventured out, people panicked, some even screamed at them telling them to go away and that they belonged in the Convent. Everyone was afraid of them, as if they were lepers. They had become outcasts. Other towns and villages refused to receive them. She said she was not possessed though she lived in continuous fear of what may befall her if she remained here.

Because of this intolerable situation and after honest consideration, she decided she wanted to leave and had arranged to get a seat on the last flight to Santa Fé that evening but was afraid if she were to appear wearing her habit she would not be allowed to board the plane. It was imperative that she change her clothes. Could Alice help her? This was the reason behind her note.

"You are about my height and weight so if you wish I can give you something to wear," offered Alice.

"You can count on me also," added Marisa. "Unless you have already arranged for transportation, I can drive you to the airport. As a matter of fact, I'll stay with you until you are safely aboard the plane."

Overcome with emotion the nun took the hands of both and pressed them with warmth of gratitude. She accepted a tissue from Marisa.

The mood in the car was interrupted by the horn blast from a car that, unnoticed by them, had pulled up next to theirs. The lady driver was motioning furiously and shouting. Unable to hear what she was saying, Raul opened his window and the screamer followed suit. "What's that nun doing out in public, get her away from us," shouted the irritate lady, an order which she underscored with less than polite arm gestures.

"Poor people, they are so frightened," commented the nun, "may God have compassion on them."

Raul revved the motor and headed for Luis' house.

CHAPTER 8

▼

Thoughts of what he had seen around the churches on his way to the office were still floating about in his mind as he went up the elevator to his office on the 5th floor of the El Clarin Building. Things were turning ugly; he wished he could do something about it, but all he had in his arsenal were words. More was needed. Damn it, he thought, someone is going to have to step forward with something soon. As he got off the elevator and headed for the door marked President, his secretary came out the door and said she would be back in a few minutes. He had three calls already, she left reminders on his desk.

The first thing he did on entering his office was to check the contents of the red box with brown vertical stripes with the word "URGENTE" emblazoned on all four sides that rested in the center of the credenza next to his desk. It was reserved for brief reports on news developments occurring during the previous evening. To his relief, he found nothing in the box that required his immediate attention.

As announced by his secretary, there were three call-reminder slips in the center of his desk. He was about to read them when his phone rang; it was his secretary telling him one of the early morning callers was on the line again, a Mr. Germán Garcia from Miami, did he want to take the call.

"Hello, this is Luis Carlos Pradilla speaking."

"*Buenos dias* Señor Pradilla, my name is Germán Garcia. I am the owner of the Clothes R-U Company here in Miami, Florida. I apologize for calling you so early but I have heard about the disturbing situation your city finds itself in. This call is about that very subject. It is about something that can help to calm the fears and anxiety that exists in your country. Are you listening Señor Pradilla?"

"Yes, but should you not be calling the city authorities rather than me?"

"No sir, you see my company and our representative in Zambilla want to place huge, and I mean real huge ads in your newspaper."

"Mr. Garcia you want to speak to our advertising department, I'll have your call transferred, but tell me in what way your advertisement will accomplish what you say it will."

"I've already spoken to your ad people and they refuse to run my advertisement. My company is ready to ship to your city from 5,000 to 11,000 T-shirts, not ordinary T-shirts mind you but T-shirts with the image of the Holy Crucifix on them. This fits in perfectly with what your people believe in and can be got at a very low price. As a matter of fact, we have about 1,000 shirts left from a Church of God conference earlier this year which have the image of Christ on them. Your people will love them. These products will go a long way towards warding off the Devil. As you can see, I know something about evil spirits and that kind of thing. Hello, hello, damn it. He hung up on me! All right, if that's the way it's going to be, we'll go with the flyers idea. We'll put flyers on the windshield of every car in that damn city including Mr. Big Shot newspaperman's."

Luis sat with elbows on his desk and head between his hands in a state of non-belief. The merchants are knocking at the gates he whispered to himself, just what the doctor ordered.

He took Garcia's call note crumpled it into a ball and threw it at the wastepaper basket. His secretary entered with his coffee, and as evidence of how well she knew her boss, she had added a little extra sugar-kick to the coffee.

"Thanks, I'm going to need all of it," as he reached for the cup she placed in front of him. He looked at the two remaining call notes and asked her to get the Director of Tourism in Santa Fe.

As she was about to leave the office the secretary turned to say she had forgotten to tell him that one of the persons who called was outside in the reception room, it was William Flores.

He said to hold the call to Santa Fe and have William come in.

Flores was one of *El Clarin's* senior reporters who came aboard a year after Luis took over the presidency. He had an uncanny ability to get behind the veneer of things and past the noise to ferret out the real story. The years had done little to diminish the verve with which he approached his work.

"William, I haven't seen you so early in the day in a long time, do you want some coffee?"

Gabriela had already offered him some, thanks. This whole city appeared to be up early and standing in front of churches. Had Luis seen what was happening out there? It was like a scene from a Kafka novel.

Yes, Luis had passed by a couple of churches on the way in.

"Well, I've spoken to some of those people, they're scared to death, some are talking about Armageddon. By the way, what happened to those women who were said to have been possessed, I don't mean the nuns but the town women. Nobody seems to know where the hell they are, no pun intended. If the authorities know, they're not opening their mouths. I'm telling you this is turning up the heat on the pressure-cooker out here."

Luis suggested Flores put someone on this to try to pry information loose. Flores might want to do it himself. Is this what he wanted to see Luis about?

No it was not, what he wanted to do was report what happened at the Bishop's residence after Luis left. One of the speakers agreed that the nuns, or at least some of them, could be examined by an independent (independent of the Church that is) psychiatrist in order to rule out the possibility that the problem is not one of demonic possession but of psychiatric disorders. In the audience was the President of the Zambilla Mental Health Institute who, as soon as the conference was over, told the Church representatives that he knew a psychiatrist who would be eminently qualified to conduct the tests. He was so confident of this that in recommending him he would do so in his capacity as President of the ZMHI. As a matter of fact, the psychiatrist he was referring to was in the audience. His name is Franz Bruef, professor of clinical psychiatry at the University of Vienna, author of a long list of books and monograms on sundry areas of psychiatry, and editor-and-chief of the professional publication *Modern Psychiatry*. Doctor Bruef informed the ZMHI President that he would be happy to be of service.

The Church representative said the idea would be considered. After some lapse the Church announced its acceptance. Doctor Bruef was at this very moment at the Convent. He will be joined by two other psychiatrists, one from the United States and another from Zambilla's Andes University.

Luis said it was good to know that something is moving along with a sense of urgency and good sense, and he assumed Flores would stay on top of developments.

"Yes, certainly, I'm on my way to the Convent right now, I've been given clearance to enter there."

"Good work, stay in touch."

Two down and one to go he thought as he rang his secretary and asked her to contact the Director of Tourism, but to first check the National Government Directory for his full name.

"Director Cabo, this is Luis Carlos Pradilla of *El Clarín* in Chucaya, I'm returning your call earlier this morning."

"Doctor (anyone of any importance in Zambilla is called *doctor*) Pradilla, I appreciate your returning my call so soon. I believe we met at the rally in Chucaya in June of 2000 for the candidacy of our president. We here in the Capital and in particular our president as well as all citizens throughout the country have been following with much concern the news about the situation in Chucaya involving the St. Agnes Convent. As your mayor has been informed, the National Government stands ready to do whatever in its power to help resolve the situation."

"Director Cabo, we appreciate your sentiments and your offer of assistance."

The Director went on to explain the reason for his call. He had been contacted by the president of a New York travel agency called Worldwide Travel Adventures. According to information obtained from reliable third-party sources, this company has a gold-plated reputation and has been in business for over 30 years. He could assure Luis that his department was meticulously careful in dealing with foreign travel agencies for there are many scams out there, a lot of fancy talk which turns out to be mere smoke, no substance. Again, this was not the case with this company, he could assure Luis.

Showing impatience, Luis said he assumed all of this was related in some way to his newspaper.

The Director said it was very much so. One of the areas of the company's expertise is in putting together travel packages to places undergoing or that have undergone some kind of disaster or catastrophe, which could be from natural causes such as hurricanes, earthquakes and volcanic eruptions as well as those resulting from human actions like prison riots, battles between military forces of small third world countries, and *coup d'etats* with public demonstrations.

"Wait a minute, just a minute, you are not about to tell me these people are proposing to send tourists here to Chucaya are you!"

No, no, no, not in the way Luis was probably imagining. The idea is to allow planes to fly over Chucaya, and in particular the Convent, and circle around for a while so that the passengers can take pictures. The planes would depart either from the Santa Fe airport or from a closer one. They will not, he repeated, will not land in Chucaya. The number of flights, the types of planes and the period over which this occur will be subject to agreement with the Director's Department and, of course, with the authorities in Chucaya. The government will be given an up-front payment of 5% of the revenues from the flights.

"Now Mr. Director…"

"Please Doctor Pradilla, with all the respect you deserve, bear with me and please hold your questions just for a moment while I finish explaining the complete proposal."

Luis pushed in the speaker phone button, placed his phone back into its cradle, moved his chair back from his desk, rested his head against the back and closed his eyes.

The Director went on to explain that it had been the company's experience that the people who go on these special tours are no penny-pinchers and always leave generous monetary reminders of having been in the places they visit. It is proposed that the Chucaya package include a two-day stay over in Santa Fe complete with hotel arrangements, cultural and shopping tours and continental breakfasts. This would be a badly needed boost to Santa Fe's economic recession. The Director had not yet contacted Chucaya's mayor but will do so that morning. What he would like from Luis' newspaper was that it publish articles calming any concerns the citizens of Chucaya may have as to the airplanes that will be flying and hovering overhead. The Government did not want the media to speculate wildly on the why of the planes. It certainly didn't want tensions aggravated, otherwise it would not hesitate to withdraw its acceptance. This will definitely be a condition of any agreement. Luis' paper being a most prestigious voice in Chucaya can play a significant role in this.

Now Luis was probably asking himself what benefit will the city of Chucaya derive from this. A good question, indeed. There will be a 10 percent surtax on all services used by the tourists and Worldwide itself, all of which will be sent to Chucaya to help cover the costs being incurred as a result of this Convent matter. Can the Director count on Luis' cooperation?

Luis remained unmoving, eyes closed.

"Doctor Pradilla, are you there? Doctor Pradilla."

The Director's sales pitch rumbled through Luis' mind, causing a surge of irritated energy to fire in all directions until converging into a single stream which vaulted directly to his mouth. "Not only will we not cooperate, we will use all the influence at our disposal to bring pressure on the National Government, including the president, to close the door to these commercial opportunists and prevent them from turning a tragic situation into an occasion for financial gain." End of conversation. He called his secretary and told her to get the Mayor, Senator Rodriguez and the Director of Civil Aeronautics on the line in that order.

While this was happening in Luis' office, back at his house Alice asked Sister Teresa whether she liked the skirt and blouse combination she was holding up for her to see. Blouses, skirts, dresses, pants and accessories covered Alice's bed.

Marisa suggested that Alice and she step out of the room for a while so that Sister Teresa could try on some of the items and make her choice.

Five minutes later the selection was completed. The nun opened her suitcase and pulled out two sets of her habit and handed them to Alice saying she would not need them any longer and did not want them found in her suitcase should it be inspected at the airport. She felt tired and facing what was sure to be a long trip back to Canada, she wanted to rest for a while.

*   *   *   *

Dr. Franz Bruef and his two assistant psychiatrists met in the confessional room at the Saint Agnes Convent. Preparations were underway for the tests that were scheduled to begin the following day. The three psychiatrists were all respected members of their profession, so it came as no surprise that they were able to quickly agree on the necessary preparations. Each was familiar with the reports on the behavior of the nuns that were made available by the Church. However, they were denied access to the findings of the Church's psychiatrists, the official explanation given was that Doctor Bruef *et al's* examination should be conducted freely and independently, uninfluenced in any way by the prior tests. The three agreed that they should test for both organic and functional psychoses such as schizophrenia, obsessive-compulsive disorders and paranoia, and that the anti-psychotic drugs chlorpromazine and haloperidol were to be available.

There was one bump along the way to agreement, it concerned the role to be played by hypnosis. Doctor Bruef was a vocal and leading proponent of the value of hypnosis in psychic diagnosis and treatment. In what was interpreted as a political effort to assert the presence and importance of the school of national psychiatry, the Zambillan member of the trio voiced a mild dissent to having the nuns subjected to hypnosis before any other diagnostic approach was tried.

The hypnosis was to be done by Doctor Bruef himself in the quiet reassuring ambience of the confessional room, in each ceiling corner of which a camera was installed that would transmit the procedure to a monitor in an adjacent room where the two colleague psychiatrists would view all that went on. A table had been set for them in which several imposing texts were lined up, some with bookmarks in place. Doctor Bruef was to wear a tiny microphone and hearing device that would allow him to remain in continuous audio contact with his colleagues.

Measures were in place to respond to any violent outburst by the nuns, a cot with attached restraining straps could be immediately rushed into service and a medical doctor and two strong men would be on standby should they be needed.

Although the Church did not in any blatant way hinder the work of the three psychiatrists, it did make decisions that were not helpful to them. There was the refusal to hand over the records on the psychiatric tests. Then at the last minute, only one of the three nuns who had exhibited the most extreme signs of disorder and who had been selected by the three psychiatrists for testing was made available. The reason given for scratching two of them from the list was that they were already undergoing preparation for exorcism.

Doctor Franz Bruef was no stranger to Church officials. They had a thick dossier on him, particularly regarding his outspoken antagonism towards the whole concept of demonic possession. The dossier included an extract from an interview he gave a year earlier to the Italian magazine *Domani*:

Questioner: How long have you been interested in demonic possession?

Bruef: At least ten years, off and on that is.

Questioner: As you know the Church, as it has made clear recently, continues to believe in demonic possession as it has over a thousand of years. Why do you believe it is wrong to do so?

Bruef: Often what people do not understand is attributed to some mysterious cause. If you combine this with the widespread ignorance of the masses centuries ago, you end up with a witch's brew hocus pocus about devils invading human bodies. Early on the Church, based on tenuous biblical references, encouraged these irrational beliefs. Once it did that and made it part of the Church's credo infrastructure it simply could not reverse itself without risking the loss of credibility of its other teachings or doctrines.

Questioner: Does modern science have an explanation for these bizarre behavioral exhibitions which the Church says are cases of demonic possession?

Bruef: We have come a long way—from a naturalistic view of disease, psychotherapy, mesmerism and to the recent use of hypnosis and specialized drugs—in building a case against these archaic beliefs. It won't be long before this whole idea of demonic possession will be relegated to the status of fairy tales, where it belongs.

Considering this, it is easy to see why the decision not to reject the selection of Bruef to head the team was not arrived at easily. In the end, the Church's conviction of the truth of the presence of demonic possession in the Convent cases was so strong that the anticipated failure of Bruef to definitively prove otherwise would be tantamount to a *coup de grace* for the Church.

∗   ∗   ∗   ∗

After third-country delays in getting through to his office, Ted was finally able to speak to several of the people in his department. No, there were no urgent matters to attend to.

Yes, the head of the Company's pension investment department had been hired away by a mutual fund but Allen Sawgrass, the second in charge, was more than able to step up and do a creditable job, at least until a permanent replacement was found.

Yes, Ted's secretary would make sure his monthly bills were paid and will have funds deposited into his checking account.

No, the semi-serious proposal that the Company consider offering demonic-possession insurance was never put on the agenda of the New Business Committee.

Yes, Ted would be e-mailed a copy of the company's proposal to acquire the Cheyenne Insurance Company.

A Mr. Paul Schaffer of Randolf Publishers called to confirm that Ted was in Chucaya and wanted to know how he could be contacted, it had something to do with writing a book.

Yes, the events in Chucaya were receiving broad media attention. They had already popped up in Jay Leno's and David Letterman's opening monologues. A number of strip joints were dressing their girls in nuns' clothing and having them do a slow bare-it-all. Supposedly, this is the latest sex fetish; the clubs were packing them in night after night.

Ted's secretary said a number of people had asked whether he was videotaping any of the things that were happening there. He had become a celebrity around the office. Was he scared at all? Could he bring her a souvenir of some kind when he returned, she would be glad to pay for it.

CHAPTER 9

▼

She could not have measured much over four feet; she looked like a child trying on her mother's clothes. Her head was shaped like a diamond, broad across the temples and forehead and narrowing almost to a point at her chin. Her face revealed both unblemished youth and premature sadness.

"Sister Maria, you have been advised that the test you are about to undergo is voluntary and that you are under no obligation whatsoever, is that correct?" stated Doctor Bruef.

"That is so."

She was seated comfortably in a soft, stuffed chair that seemed incongruous in the sparse simplicity of the room. It had been brought to the Convent especially for the test. Directly in front of her sat Doctor Bruef in a metal folding chair, wearing brown slacks and a tieless darker brown shirt, purposely selected to create a casual, relaxed setting. There was a conscious absence of anything in the room that might attract her attention away from the doctor.

The combination of his reassuring avuncular manner and the soft tone of his voice were designed to convince her that he meant only good and that he could be trusted. The ultimate aim was to put her conscious mind into an inactive state, allowing the doctor to access her subconscious.

He began by asking her personal questions; her name, place of birth, early childhood experiences all of which were covered in the bio-sheet the Church had provided. The questions were selected and then framed in such a way as to evoke pleasant, or at least emotionally neutral, responses.

The nun's answers soon began to reflect an increasing ease. Before bringing her into a full trance, Doctor Bruef tested her willingness and capacity to be fully hypnotized. This he did by at first asking her to make certain movements, followed by suggestions that required her to suspend disbelief or to distort normal thoughts.

At first, the nun readily followed all the suggestions but then rebellion crept in. "Slowly raise your right arm and touch the crown of your head." She began to raise her arm but as she was about to touch her head the arm jerked back to its original position.

He repeated the instruction adding, "Touch your head and leave your hand there until I tell you to lower it." Again she completed half of the instruction then dropped her arm.

Changing his approach he whispered, "Sister Maria you are completely relaxed, your arms have no weight, they are like feathers, feel how they want to float in the air." Her arms began to rise in feather-like motion only to abruptly fall.

Doctor Breuf whispered into his microphone that her behavior was perplexing. She evidenced signs of threshold hypnosis but there seemed to be an inner layer obstructing access to her subconscious. He was not getting through.

The whispered voice of one of the colleagues suggested he might try to get her subconscious to understand that there's interference, an obstacle of some kind. Why didn't he try to…then loud static. Doctor Breuf removed his earphone, gave it a gentle shake and put it back to his ear. The static noise was now even louder. Then the monitor in the adjoining room went blank. Unaware of the totality of the communications breakdown, Doctor Breuf looked in the direction of one of the cameras, pointed to the earphone and gave a "not-working" gesture and turned back to the nun.

"Sister Maria, you in peeeace, listen to the sound of gentle streeeams, feel the fresh softness of the breeze upon your face, relax, let goooo you are the streeeam, you are the breeze, listen to…" A fierce stabbing hit his ear from the earphone and fired through his brain, the cameras in the four corners began whirling. He tore the earphone from his ear and was about to cry out in pain when the nun in one seamless rapid motion lifted her skirt, raised her bent legs to the level of her breast and delivered a kick to the doctor's chest with such extraordinary force that it lifted him out of his chair and propelled him across the room, smack against the wall and then to the floor in a daze.

The nun made a low rumbling noise then sat back unmoving except for a quivering that appeared in different parts of her body as if something were traveling around under her skin. She opened her mouth wide and disgorged a putrid odor that spread across the room. Doctor Breuf began to gag.

The two assistant psychiatrists hearing the loud sounds from the room, rushed to open the door only to back away as the stench reached their nostrils. Holding handkerchiefs over their mouths and noses and with the help of the two strong-men, they got Doctor Breuf onto a stretcher and removed him from the room. Turning to the nun they quickly set up a cot and strapped her into it. At first, she offered no resistance but then began to writhe and pull against the restraining straps.

The preliminary opinion of the medical doctor was that Doctor Bruef had suf-fered several broken ribs, a dislocated right shoulder, a fractured femoral bone of the left leg and lacerations. With speed never before witnessed in the Convent, he was placed on a gurney and into an ambulance that sped to the Chucaya hospital.

With the air now cleaner, a nurse prepared an injection needle with enough potent tranquilizer/sedative to reduce the ranging bull into a sheep. As the doctor and the nurse approached, the nun struggled violently against the leather straps, her bulging eyes followed their every movement. With the support of the two muscled helpers, her right arm was immobilized and the drug injected.

"My God," shouted the nurse, "look there," as she pointed to the arm. Large pores opened along the extension of the right arm out of which a yellowish liquid was oozing. Those in the room touched each other in disbelief. The doctor handed one of the men a ball of cotton and asked him to wipe some of the liquid from her arm.

Sniffing the cotton, the doctor's face became a maze of perplexity. To verify the accuracy of his conclusion, he sniffed the vial from which he had drawn the injected drug. He looked at the two psychiatrists and his nurse and holding out the cotton ball proclaimed, "This is the sedative-tranquilizer I just injected into her vein."

"Not possible," said the psychiatrists almost in unison. "Do you mind letting me smell them," asked one of them. Then shaking his head in disbelief, he handed the ball to the second psychiatrist.

The silence in the room was broken by a soft, gentle female voice that expressed a different kind of surprise. "What happened, why am I strapped to this bed," asked Sister Maria.

*   *   *   *

Embraces, thank you and best wishes exchanged, Alice and Marisa watched Teresa Robbins—the former Sister Teresa—walk down the tube-corridor to the waiting plane. "She made it, didn't she," sighed Alice.

"I suppose we could say we all made it," smiled Marisa.

There was mostly silence in the car on the way back to Luis' house as both women thought about the fast-paced, grainy events of the day. Alice broke the silence by saying she had been entertaining an idea that seemed kind of nutty even to her at first, but it just would not go away, it had taken a stubborn grip on her imagination. She wanted to share it with Marisa if she didn't mind.

"You have piqued my curiosity my dear friend, but to tell you the truth, considering everything that's happened recently I can't see how anything you tell me will come as a shock, so go ahead, my mind is cleared to receive your every word."

"Do you agree that we're all being kept in the dark as to what's really going on in the Convent, no news, no reports and that all we've been told is that priests will be conducting exorcisms, right. But we really don't know, do we."

"Agreed, but nothing you've said so far can be considered even moderately jolting."

"Do you agree that Sister Teresa and I are about the same height?"

"Well, yes I guess so, but so are you and I."

"I want to enter the Convent. I want to see with my own two curious eyes what's happening, I want to go in there.

"Not much of a chance of that happening, you know no one can enter that place except Church and medical people. The road to the Convent is closed to all but approved vehicles. And even if you trudge your way through the woods and manage to get there, you won't be allowed in, that's for certain. I am sure you know all this."

"Nuns are Church people are they not, I'm sure they will be allowed in."

"Now you've lost me."

"Why can't I put on Sister Teresa's habit, one of those she left with us, and go there as a nun."

There was silence. Marisa kept her eyes on the road, wondering whether this woman's synapses were misfiring. She would never get away with it. She was bound to be found out. Yet, the idea did have an aura of intrigue about it.

"You haven't commented, what do you think?"

"Mission impossible, and if successful loaded with risk and uncertainty as to what could happen once inside."

"I can do it. I won't stay there long, just enough to get an idea of what's going on." She said this with a slight passing chill as she remembered she used these same words before departing for Israel to get information on the Palestine situation and just missed getting blown to smithereens.

"But you don't speak Spanish."

"Neither does Sister Teresa."

"And Ted, how do you intend to handle him. He's going to resist you all the way on this."

"I can manage him, and anyway he doesn't run my life."

Two hours later in the patio of Luis' house a flustered Ted Shaw walked back and forth with short, hurried steps, waiving indecipherable patterns in the air with agitated arms.

"Alice, this is the peak, the zenith, why in heaven's name are you so fixed on exposing yourself to danger. Isn't there enough of it out there already without you going out and stirring up even more? You could end up in jail or worse. This is not the United States you know. This whole thing is not our problem and it certainly isn't your problem. You've heard what happened to that German or Austrian or whatever psychiatrist at the Convent haven't you? He'll never recover from his ordeal."

Alice felt like a child being admonished by her father. She refused to flinch and argued back her cause calmly but with determination. While depictions of horrific consequences, supplications, pleadings to rationality were whirling around, Luis entered the patio having just arrived home.

Upon seeing him, Ted rushed over and asked that he help talk sense to into Alice. Distraught, Ted turned to Marisa—who during all of the discussions had sat quietly, trying to give the impression she was not listening—for an explanation. Not waiting for her response, he told Alice to explain her wacky idea. Bemused by the scene playing out before him, Luis asked Marisa to explain.

"Isn't the idea ridiculous," said Ted after Marisa had finished, "you tell her Luis, she won't listen to me."

"For heavens sake Ted," complained Alice, "we are guests here in Luis' home, we're not here to unload our differences on him. Now come on, you're just not being fair to him."

"Luis is my friend, and this is what friends do for each other."

Luis raised his arms to request calm and said there was clearly a huge danger and risk in carrying out Alice's plan which, incidentally, might even be a violation of recently issued decrees regarding the Convent situation.

"See there," shouted out Ted, "it's worse than even I imagined."

Luis said it would be a risky adventure for a young lady like Alice to be out there on her own. There was a great deal of tension and confusion in the city.

"She won't be alone, if she will let me, I'll go with her, Sister Teresa left two complete habits behind," interjected Marisa.

Alice ran to Marisa and hugged her; the two men stood looking at each other. "I can't believe this," remarked Ted.

Luis raised his hand again asking for calm. It was clear the women could not be dissuaded from their intended folly, so the four should do all possible to reduce the risk of something going wrong. He suggested everyone take time to cool off, perhaps they could have dinner out together later that evening.

There was little discussion between the two American visitors following the patio episode up until the couples ordered their pre-dinner drinks at the Papagallo restaurant. During that interval the firestorm set off in Ted's mind by Alice's announcement had calmed down to occasional gusts:

"Are you sure you've thought this out," or, "you might get caught and there's no American consulate in the city," then a suggestion of long-term consequences, "this could result in your getting a police record," followed by recourse to a different center of concern, "you know I'll be going through tremendous stress while you're gone."

In response to Ted's mildly calmer attitude, Alice toned down her earlier aggressiveness. She assured Ted that she would be careful, and would back away from any engagement with the authorities, for she and Marisa will be there as observers and not as interlopers.

There were only two other couples in the Papagallo restaurant when Luis' quartet arrived. Though initially a little stiff, conversation gradually loosened up somewhat with the aid of the two bottles of the restaurant owner's favorite Proseco wines. Inevitably, the subject of the Convent venture came up and an agreement was reached on a number of points: the women would be driven to the Convent by Luis' chauffer; neither Ted nor Luis would accompany them so as not to raise questions or suspicions; Marisa was to a carry cell-phone; the maximum time they were to spend in the Convent was six hours; upon leaving Luis' house the women would wear civilian dress over their nun habits.

Though a far cry from the excitement and agitation that had domain a few hours earlier and despite the accord on the ground rules for the Convent visit, there were still prickly traces of tension in the air. In an attempt to divert thoughts to a different and more congenial topic, Alice turned to Luis and Marisa and asked how long they had known each other, where were they born and did they both grow up in Chucaya.

Caught off balance by the sudden transition to a new subject, one having no discernable connection to the discussions up to that point and, moreover, concerning a personal relationship, there was a clearing of throats that really required no clearing and a reaching for wine glasses that did need emptying.

Ted tapped Alice's leg under the table in a sign of opposition and testily said, "Now Alice, I don't..." when he was cut short by Luis who said he was not at all surprised that Alice should wonder about the nature of the relationship between Marisa and him, after all they hadn't said a word about it. At least he had not.

In a sign of confidentiality, Luis drew his chair closer to the table and said that Marisa and he had known each other for many years. Explaining their relationship in a few sentences was something neither one of them felt capable of doing. Turning to Marisa in a gentle tone, he added that perhaps the occasion of this evening, with the thought in mind of what will be transpiring over the next few days and considering the warm congeniality that had arisen among the four of them, Marisa and he should share their story with Ted and Alice. Did Marisa agree?

Marisa, who during this time had been studying the wine in her glass that she tipped from side to side, causing it to shift in waves, said she had no objection.

Luis ordered another bottle of Proseco, smiled and began by saying that before getting to Marisa and him, he had to first relate a story that occurred long ago which would help put things into clearer perspective.

Years ago Chucaya was an insular town with only the barest of contact with the rest of the country. Local transportation was by horseback or carriage. There were two ways to reach Santa Fe, one was by the once-a-week train or aboard a steamer on the River Magda. As anyone who had any knowledge of this part of the world would expect, society in that Chucaya was characterized by a rigid tri-layered class stratification. The pinnacle was occupied by long-established families that owned what was at that time the most important source of wealth, land. They were universally recognized as the elite of society. Below them came the small group of professionals and merchants, what would by present day standards be considered an incipient middle class. The bottom strata, the most densely populated of the three, was comprised almost exclusively of the native Indian population.

Taking advantage of the fact the waiter brought a fresh bottle of wine to the table and began serving it, Alice commented that what Luis was describing resembled something out of the 1700s. Marisa said that in fact it was set in the late eighteen hundreds.

"You know, I would have liked to have lived back then, said Ted, "it must have been a tranquil and orderly world with few uncertainties, a kind of age of predictability unlike the one we're living in now."

"But I don't suppose it was that great for the native Indians," observed Alice. "I'm sorry Luis, please go on."

Luis continued.

There was no university in Chucaya, which meant that the elite families either sent their children to the Universidad de Santo Tomas in Santa Fe or to one in Europe. This was the expected thing, so it came as no small shock to Amadeo when his 19 year old son Enrique informed him he did not want to attend any university at all, and that he preferred to remain in Chucaya to help his father with the administration of his properties. Enrique was unshakable in his resolve even in the face of pleadings and offers of rewards. Now this was a serious matter back then, for the authority and wishes of a father were not something one would lightly challenge.

Suspecting an ulterior motive on his son's part, Amadeo began snooping around and learned that Enrique had been seen with a local Indian girl on several occasions. Intent on finding out all he could regarding this, the father set about having the allegation fully investigated. The report he got back confirmed what he had been told and his worse fears. The girl, whose name was Naomi, was the 16 year old daughter of an Indian woman who worked for a Felucio Morandi, the Italian owner of a local printing office. There was no information on the father, though there was speculation that it may have been the Italian himself. Naomi was said to be startlingly beautiful.

Confronted with this information Enrique offered no denial but rather said that they were in love. And so began the second acrimonious confrontation in just a few days. How could he be so ridiculous, so immature. Did he understand what this would do to the family's reputation, a reputation not obtained overnight but earned over many decades. It was the greatest asset a man could have. What is a man without his reputation, a nobody who occupies space and no more. To allow a gossamer thing like romance to prevail over sound family and social values and in the process stain the family reputation made less than no sense at all, it was disgraceful. And on and on continued the father while the son listened impassively.

Was it sex, then get it but don't fool-headedly mix in romance. If Enrique wished, the father would hire the girl to work in the household, she would be paid well and Enrique would have access to her whenever he wanted and until he got tired of her. This would hurt no one.

"You just don't understand do you father, how demeaning can you be," shouted an angry Enrique as he turned and left the room. The father's face flushed with anger. He clenched his fists.

A waiter came to the table to tell Luis he had a telephone call in the manager's office. Asking Marisa to continue the narrative, Luis headed for his telephone call with the let-down feeling one experiences when forced to discontinue a pleasing activity for one of potential aggravation.

"You know," said Alice, "the father, what's his name…"

"Amadeo," filled in Marisa.

"Oh, yes, Amadeo, well how low can one get, how absolutely cynical to suggest bringing the girl into the house as a sex plaything for the son. Dehumanizing."

"Remember, at that time the demarcation between social classes was very clearly drawn and as one descended down the scale there was a corresponding loss of human identity. The emphasis on preserving the status of the family name was a bastion against the blurring and eroding of class distinctions. But let me continue on from where Luis left off, that is if you're still interested in this long narrative in answer to your simple question."

"Please, of course, sorry I interrupted you," apologized Alice.

Marisa continued.

A few weeks after the father/son confrontation the Italian was found dead, shot in the left temple. A perfunctory police investigation concluded it was a suicide though no gun was ever found and despite the fact the Italian was right-handed.

Naomi's mother attempted to continue operating the printing business of which she had learned much from the Italian. So her failure in the end was due less to her inability than to the lack of customers, something in which Enrique's father had much to do.

When the printing business failed Noami and her mother left town. A few months later Naomi gave birth to a daughter.

Enrique made every effort to locate Naomi with no success. She wrote letters which, with the collusion in the post office, never reached Enrique. So they went unanswered leading her to believe he had lied to her and was never in love as he had professed. Naomi stopped writing. Enrique, hurt by the fact she had not communicated with him, shared her feelings about having been lied to and gave up looking for her.

Naomi and her mother went to live in a town some 200 miles from Chucaya where the mother's aunt lived. A few years later Naomi met and married a local school teacher who immediately took an interest in Naomi's daughter's education. Through his mentorship the child earned one academic award after another all the way to the University of St. Thomas in Santa Fe.

In an effort to overcome his depression over having lost Naomi, Enrique spent a year at the Universita di Bologna in Italy. There he met a Spanish exchange student who he eventually married. The couple returned to Chucaya where they made their home. They had one son, who later attended the University of St. Thomas in Santa Fe.

It was there that the Enrique's son and Naomi's daughter met.

At the point Marisa stopped talking, causing Ted to ask whether that was the end of the story, and Alice to ask what happened to the students, did Marisa know them.

"Do I know them, well, yes I do, as a matter of fact the former student and son of Enrique is heading for our table at this moment."

Ted and Alice turned to look, it was Luis. Alice pointed to Marisa and said "and you're Naomi's daughter."

"From your expressions, it looks like Marisa has reached the end of the tale," smiled Luis as he reached the table.

Alice could not contain herself. "What an incredibly touching story, I mean, if you overlook the first part," then pausing for a moment said, "but then if we did that the rest of the story would lose its drama, I guess."

"Then you and Marisa are, how can I put it…"

"It's all right, I understand what's troubling you about this, Marisa and I have obviously asked ourselves your unfinished question. We don't know whether we are brother and sister, at least half so, or whether we are, what's the word I'm looking for, oh yes, or whether we are my father Enrique's and Marisa's mother Naomi's proxies or surrogates playing out the relationship that was cruelly not allowed to continue to its natural conclusion."

"But…" began Alice, then shaking her head, "I'm getting to personal."

For the first time since Ted and Alice arrived in Chucaya, Marisa openly showed affection towards Luis and placed her hand on his and said she could probably foretell the question Alice was about to ask. Yes, it was true, she didn't know who had fathered her, was it Enrique or was it the Italian, or perhaps someone else. Also, who killed the Italian? She was sure he had not committed suicide and it was absurd to contend otherwise. From what she had been told, he was a happy person who had achieved long-worked-for business success, moreover, he was awaiting the visit of his brother from Italy, the expenses for which he had happily agreed to underwrite. There was no evidence to support a finding of suicide.

Luis said it was his turn to anticipate their next and very logical question as he caressed Marisa's hand. Why he had not turned to modern science to resolve the paternity question, DNA, etc. The practical answer was that his father Enrique passed away years ago, the body cremated and the ashes scattered over his land. Luis acknowledged that what he had just said was probably a rationalization. What was true was that Marisa and he preferred to leave things undisturbed, to do otherwise would deprive their relationship of a certain mystique that exists in the attraction of the uncertain. But it went beyond that, it had to do with a certain intractable unwillingness to have one of their dual relationships terminated since both gave them great pleasure and happiness. Call it a natural, tenacious drive for psychic or relationship-survival.

"Look at it this way," added Marisa, "doesn't everyone desire to enjoy one's life experience, the only one he or she will ever have, in a way that is as all embracing and inclusive and as multi-dimensional as possible. You can say that Luis and I have been given precisely such an opportunity. We accept this as a unique gift to us."

"What a touching and intriguing story," commented Alice in a low tone as if what had been revealed had to be sheltered from extraneous ears.

Ted wanted to know how they were able to handle the matter of their uncertain relationship, for the two relationships didn't involve the same behavior towards each other.

"Let's say we have found a satisfactory *modus vivendi,* a way to not only accommodate both of them but also to have them grow and flourish."

*   *   *   *

Across the country at the home of the President of Zambilla a maid entered the library, "Señor Presidente, Señor Ildefonso Pruz has arrived."

"Have him come in," said Mariano Corvina Montes, President of Zambilla as he looked up from a report that had been handed him that afternoon by the Director of Communications regarding the proposal received from Worldwide Travel Adventures. As he put the report down, he thought the country could surely use additional revenues.

Señor Pruz entered with hand extended and walked toward the president. "My dear Ildefonso," cordially greeted the president as he stood up and stepped to the side of his desk to embrace the Chairman of the Liberal Party, a long-time political crony. "Please sit and tell me how is Carmen Rosa and your children."

"They are fine, thank you. I wish to apologize for disturbing you at home but I felt the subject I wish to bring up with you is delicate and best discussed in the privacy of your home. I will not abuse your kindness in receiving me at this hour and will be as brief as possible."

"Please, there is no need to apologize, you know you are always welcome here at any hour."

The chairman nodded in appreciation. "As is widely known our economy is ailing from this yearlong recession, we have a zero gross domestic product which threatens to soon show negative growth, unemployment is zooming. Our citizens are clamoring for the government to take some action. The local press is hammering us on a daily basis. On top of all of this, the International Monetary Fund is pressing us to adopt even more stringent—I would go so far as to say draconian—economic measures as a prerequisite to considering rolling over our debt which is soon coming due for repayment. But who knows more about this than you, sitting as you do in the center of this maelstrom."

The president straightened up in his chair and said that the government had adopted strong measures to correct this situation and that it took time for the effects of these measures to work their way through the economy.

The chairman knew this to be the case, but the ordinary citizen, the common man in his poncho, was impacted more directly by the immediate situation and he thought in terms of today and not of a promised future. Hunger is always felt in the present.

Presidential elections would soon be upon them and the tendency of voters will be to blame the Liberal Party for what's happening. The government must identify some issue, some matter different from the economy to which the people's attention can be diverted, one around which they can wrap themselves and, most importantly, to which this government can be linked in a positive way.

"Señor Chairman, you and I are on the same political wavelength for I have come to the same conclusion. Do you have any ideas about what can serve as an effective diversion, of course I have my own ideas about this but I would appreciate hearing about yours."

"We have been handed just such an opportunity. I refer to what has been occurring at the convent in Chucaya which I understand has spread not only beyond that convent but also beyond Chucaya. People around the country are concerned, actually in some locations they are frightened. Personally, I am of the opinion that this is more a question of psychology, of auto-suggestion and such rather than having anything to do with demons and evil spirits. I'm no expert on these matters but my sense of things tells me this is not what it is being portrayed to be."

"You may have found the answer which, incidentally, I too have considered." The president showed the chairman the report from the Secretary of Communications saying he had just received a report on the demons matter, but to please continue.

"I must now be totally frank with you for as I have said or at least have strongly intimated, our party's fate in the next election hangs in the balance. We must not only hope that this demons thing continues but we, as lifelong devoted members of the Liberal Party, are obliged to see that it does continue and with increasing intensity, at least until after the elections. Most importantly, the government must come off as a concerned government and seen as doing all it can to resolve, or whatever one does, to end this demon scare. Let me be clear. I am here as a messenger of the party, the key members of which advocate what I have just said. The details on how your government can accomplish what at times seems like contradictory objectives, we leave to your well-tested and trusted political savvy.

The following day the president convened an Extraordinary Meeting of Ministers to consider the situation. According to the minutes of the meeting after the president reviewed the situation of the Chucaya nuns, there was a feeling of uncertainty as to what the government could do in what was basically a Church matter, though at the same time it was acknowledged that the repercussions were beginning to be felt in different spheres of secular activities in Zambilla.

The Minister of Justice pointed out there were no precedents in the country's history for this phenomenon. A suggestion by the Minister of Interior that the president use his constitutional power to declare a State of Emergency was quickly rejected out of concern it would be adding fuel to a fire and could turn fear into panic. Moreover, the nation was facing neither a military nor economic crises which was what a State of Emergency Declaration was intended to address. What it faced was a non-material, invisible enemy, one which is the domain of those spiritual leaders who had the required knowledge and experience to deal with this type of phenomenon.

Two resolutions were approved: A special committee comprised of government, academic and religious leaders would be set up to study the situation which would then report back directly to the president with recommendations. An emergency office was to be set up in the Presidential Palace to process all requests for financial and other assistance received from Church officials in connection with efforts to deal with the crisis.

Over the next few days several ministers quietly sent their daughters out of the country ostensibly for educational reasons. In doing so they were following the lead of the country's affluent parents. President Mariano Corvina Montes made several telephone calls to media industry leaders about the government's intention to work with Church officials to resolve the Convent problem. He also placed a call to the Director of Tourism instructing him to contact Worldwide Tours to work out a draft agreement for him to review. What better way, he thought, was there to keep this nun thing alive and at the same time add to the treasury's coffers.

CHAPTER 10

▼

Having returned from the Papagallo restaurant, the two couples were relaxing with a cognac-coffee when Inga, the elderly maid, entered the room and addressed Luis.

"Señor Pradilla, I wish to request permission to absent myself from the house tomorrow morning starting at 8 a.m. I am sorry I cannot give you an exact time of my return, but it should not be much later than three in the afternoon. Forgive me for the lateness of this request but it was not more than an hour ago that I learned about my need to leave."

Inga had been an efficient and trusted servant for many years and seldom made special requests for time off, so Luis figured it must be an urgent matter of importance that required her leaving on such a short notice.

"Of course you may go, I hope it's not any personal or family emergency."

"No Señor, it is that I have been told about a ceremony the Hijos will be having in which I am very interested."

"Is this related to what has happened at the Convent?"

She hesitated for a moment, "Si, Señor."

After the maid left the room, Marisa explained to the two Americans that the maid belonged to the "Children of the Sun" who were usually referred to as the "Hijos," composed exclusively of native Indians. The group's mission was to preserve and pass on what remained of the cultural heritage of the Incas, particularly certain traditional belief systems and rituals that revolve around their gods, especially the highest of all, Inki or Sun god. It seems they will be conducting one of their ritual ceremonies tomorrow from what Inga told Luis.

Ted asked if this was some kind of occultism or voodooism. Marisa confessed she didn't know much about those practices but suspected they were mostly unrelated. She had been to several of the Hijos ceremonies and there certainly weren't any sticking of needles in dolls.

If Ted's customary reactions could be described in one word it would be "predictable," which is why Alice could hardly believe her ears when she heard him ask whether it would be possible to attend the next day's ceremony as an observer. This about-face attitude was no slip of the tongue, but neither was it because Ted was particularly interested in rituals. It was more remedial in nature than anything else, an attempt to impress on Alice that he was not adverse to all new experiences and consequently that their drifting apart was not necessarily inevitable. Either not having heard or understood the maid's answer to Luis' question regarding the connection to the Convent, Ted felt that by attending the Hijos' ceremony Alice's attention might be diverted from the Convent folly.

For the first time in a while Alice found herself supporting one of Ted's activity suggestions. Seizing upon this rare occasion of rapport, Marisa went immediately to Inga to see if Ted's wish could be realized, though she had reservations about a person like Ted attending what she knew would be sacred Indian ceremonies.

Yes, the Americans could go as observers provided Marisa accompanied them and that throughout the ceremonies they maintained absolute silence. Marisa was familiar with the place where the event was to take place. Agreed, departure time 8 a.m.

The sky was sagging under heavy grayness as the trio stepped up and into the well-traveled jeep that Luis provided. Marisa was in the driver's seat. Ted was curious why such a brawny vehicle, where were they traveling to?

"It's about 70 kilometers in that direction," indicated Marisa with a nod of her head as she put the gearshift into first, "about half of the way will be over bumpy, unpaved roads." Her head motion had indicated they would be traveling parallel to the mountain range, the direction from which the sun rose in the morning.

A few kilometers later, Ted asked of whether they were going to another town or what.

Marisa explained that it was a sort of a town centuries ago, but all that remains today, as they would soon see, are a few walls that have managed to withstand the ravages of time and weather, a few vaulting renaissance doorways, bell towers that valiantly struggle against intruding date palms and the facades of a couple of convents."

"Does or did it have a name?"

"Santiago de La Vega."

"Sounds like real heavy Spanish, right out of a history book."

Alice had been sitting quietly looking out at the passing landscape lost in her thoughts when Marisa's description of the place they were heading to penetrated the veil around her reverie.

"I'll wager there's a great story about what happened to Santiago de La Vega," she said.

"Knowing what I know, I respectfully reject your offer to wager," smiled Marisa.

"Here's the dirt road you mentioned," said Ted as the vehicle began bumping along and shifting its passengers from side to side.

Marisa explained that during colonial times Santiago de La Vega was one of the richest regions in what is now Zambilla, host to vast sugar plantations that became important exporters to the whole world. Powerful families of Spanish descent built huge haciendas there. So wealthy were they that it was not unusual to find the women dressed in the latest fashions from Europe. Mansions were furnished with the finest tapestries from around the world, walls were adorned with valuable paintings and floors covered with rugs imported from the Middle East. In short, opulent splendor was everywhere.

"Sorry, I didn't see that one," as the vehicle ran in and out of a sizeable pothole, "we are getting close now, it's just beyond those corn fields."

She went on to explain that word of La Vega's wealth and opulence circulated widely even abroad and it was this that brought about its undoing. It was in the late 1600s that La Vega was plundered by the English pirate Edward David and all of its objects of wealth carried away. The plantation owners and their families abandoned the town. A few months later the town was destroyed by ravaging flood waters.

According to legend, the destruction of La Vega was brought about by the gods as punishment for the evil that flourished there following its sacking by the English pirate. Blacks, mulattos and others who had worked in the sugar plantations had taken over the town once the plantation owners left and, it was said, turned it into a center of eroticism and debauchery. Since that time the ruins of La Vega have been considered to be a place where evil spirits continue to inhabit.

The natives believe that by celebrating religious rites there they are appealing to the gods to protect the people against new evils. A strange twist of logic but, again, religious beliefs are seldom on speaking terms with logic and reason are they?

"What do you expect will happen there today, any idea?" asked Alice.

"The natives have a whole repertoire of rites and rituals. I can't tell what they will be doing, and I neglected to ask Inga about it. But you should bear in mind that in the spiritual culture of the natives as well as that of their ancestors there is a deep reverence for nature and its products including natural formations. It will be no surprise to see this reflected in what we are about to see.

*   *   *   *

A meeting was underway in the office of the Bishop of Chucaya. In attendance were the Bishop, the diocese Secretary, Father Giovanni, his assistant/protégé Father Russo, and two other representatives from the Vatican, Fathers Pierre and Sevilla. The meeting had been called at the request of Father Giovanni for the purpose of reviewing the ground rules for the exorcism. If he had had his way he would not have invited the Bishop—though under normal situations it was the local Bishop who had to authorize an exorcism—for experience had taught him that outsiders were more of a hindrance than anything else. But the Vatican, in superceding the Bishop's authority in this case, required that he be permitted to sit in on the meeting. What role he was to have would be up to Father Giovanni, who had already decided it would be minimal at best.

"Have you seen these," asked Father Sevilla, holding up a white T-shirt imprinted with the facial image of Jesus framed against an oval yellow background. On the back was the message that "Jesus Saves." Father Sevilla said these were being sold all around town. He saw one that said, "Down with the Devil."

The Bishop, in order not to appear to be out of touch with what was happening in his own diocese's backyard, said he knew of these and that apparently they came from Miami. There wasn't much he could do about them.

The Secretary said that the Bishop in Santa Fe had received a call from the Miami exporter asking whether he was willing to bless these articles in bulk at the airport upon their clearing customs. This, he said, would not only make the shirts more effective but would help in marketing them. He would happily donate five percent from the sales proceeds to the Bishop's diocese.

"The Bishop of Santa Fe is a holy servant of God," pointed out the Secretary. "But admittedly, he has his moments of what I would characterize not as anger but rather as excessive frustration and his reaction to the request was less, let us say, than charitable. Now we find that local distributors have been approaching individual churches to have bundles of these articles blessed."

The Bishop interrupted to point out that a letter has gone out to all diocese churches with instructions to turn down all such requests.

"*Spiritu Comercio* is well and thriving in Chucaya," commented Father Russo."

Of course I understand how taxing all of this is but it is not a matter that concerns our group here today, unless in some way it materially interferes with our work," observed Father Giovanni, "so let us move on to the items to be discussed here this morning. Father Russo please proceed."

The Bishop of Santa Fe doesn't get angry! What a distortion thought Father Russo. Everyone knows he has a nasty temper and a sharp tongue to go with it, so why this lip charade. Cardinal Hernandez has spoken to the Bishop on more than one occasion about his uncontrolled temper.

Clearing these thoughts from his mind, Father Russo proceeded to run down the list of items on the agenda. One hour and twenty minutes later the meeting ended having reached a decision on each item:

a.   All exorcisms are to take place in the Convent.

b.   Commencing with the close of this meeting and up to the time all exorcisms have been completed, decisions regarding matters pertaining to the Convent shall be made by Father Giovanni and his accompanying exorcist priests.

c.   Only a select five lay persons will be allowed to observe the exorcism. They are to be picked by Father Pierre from a list of ten submitted by the Bishop.

d.   After a prolonged discussion it was agreed that the optimum chance of success against the multiple and proliferating cases of demonic possession would be to conduct the exorcism on the person who gave the clearest indication of being the fountainhead source of all the possessions. The theory underlying this decision was that a number of Satanic spirits are involved in the possessions occurring at the Convent and that they are acting under the influence of Satan who had himself taken over the fountainhead. Based on all the information available to those at the meeting, it was believed that Sister Dolores des Agnes, the abbess of the Convent, was the fountainhead.

e.   Father Giovanni will conduct the exorcism and Father Russo will be his assistant. Also present in the exorcism room will be: a member of Sister

Dolores' family, if available, if not, then a person in whom she has confidence and trust; a medical doctor who is familiar with her medical history; Father Pierre who, together with the doctor, will remain out of immediate sight; Father Sevilla will be with the five lay observers to explain events as they occur.

f.   On the eve of the exorcism, those—except for Sister Dolores—who will be present in the exorcism room will gather in that same room and undergo spiritual purification, which will include continuous confessions. Following this, the group will remain together in joint sleeping quarters until the exorcism begins the following morning. On the morning of the exorcism, they will attend a special mass exclusively for them to be said by the Bishop.

g.   The Bishop will meet with Sister Dolores and invite her to participate in what he will refer to as a spiritual exercise. Refusal on her part will result in forced submission, the arrangements for which will be left to Father Sevilla. Her voluntary cooperation will be preferred.

h.   Once the exorcism begins and until concluded, under no circumstances shall there be any communication with the outside world nor shall anyone in the room attempt to communicate verbally with the exorcist. The exorcism is not to be interrupted under any circumstances, unless done so by the exorcist himself.

No date was fixed for the exorcism, Father Giovanni would do that.

*   *   *   *

Ted, Alice and Marisa made their way through the *ad hoc* parking lot occupied mostly by old model pick-up trucks and Fords sporting different degrees of rust and corrosion. At the head stood a brightly multicolored mini-bus.

"There are a good number of people here," pointed out Marisa as her arm made a sweeping motion over the parked vehicles.

Ted said the last time he saw such oldies was in a movie about the 1950s, there were not many of these still around in the States let alone on the roads. "I bet none of these are covered by extended warranties, wouldn't you say Alice?"

"Actually, with some repair work and a good paint job they could be real gems, I would love to have one myself," announced Alice.

Detecting the imminence of another outbreak of cross-current friction between the two Americans, Marisa interjected the explanation that the people attending these types of ceremonies are, for the most part, natives from not only Chucaya but from the surrounding villages. What the Americans were looking at was all that these people can afford.

"I can see some ruins straight ahead beyond those trees," said Alice excitedly, "look there's some kind of entrance to something."

What she was looking at was the arched façade of what local historians say was the Convent of San Francisco, one of the most architecturally beautiful of the several convents once found in La Vega.

"The bricks used in its construction were so solidly made and fitted that it was said that the gods must have have imparted special knowledge to the builders," pointed out Marisa.

As the trio reached the other side of the line of trees, the vista of what remained of La Vega opened up before their eyes exactly as Marisa had depicted it; broken stone walls that once marked off boundaries, solitary archways, sides of what were once stone buildings of some kind, fragments of roads, bell towers and throughout, trees, grass and shrubs conspiring to return the area to its original state in nature.

The entire area was enclosed within a circle of trees causing Alice to comment that this natural phenomenon seemed to have the purpose of preserving and protecting it from the outside world. The view made her skin tingle with excitement and wonder, and for a few moments encouraged her imagination to run free and picture La Vega as the flourishing center of opulence that it once was.

Ted observed that if these properties had been insured by a local insurance company it probably would have been thrown into bankruptcy.

Pointing to the far end where a group of people was gathered, Marisa said that was probably where the ceremonies were to take place. As they headed towards the gathering, they ran into three men standing with arms folded across their chests blocking the path and leaving little of their intent to guesswork. Marisa stepped forward a couple of paces and was about to address them when Inga, Luis' maid, came up from behind the three men and said something to them in a language completely strange to Alice and Ted. Two of the men reluctantly stepped aside and then left while the third defiantly stood his ground. Inga motioned Marisa and the Americans to step around the lone self-appointed sentry.

Pointing to a raised ground at the edge of a circular area where people were congregated, Inga told Marisa that she and her American friends were to go there, from where they would be able to view the ceremonies. Once these began, they must maintain absolute silence, no moving around, or they will be removed. "Senorita Marisa, remember you have been allowed to be here only because of me. You know about our ceremonies and how harsh it will be on me if you are forced to leave. If you want to explain something to the Americanos whisper very low, please."

Having completed her exhortations, Inga turned, placed a huge amulet around her neck and descended into the gathering below.

The natives sat on the ground in two semi-circles six people deep, one of men and one of women. At first faintly detectable but gradually swelling louder came the sound of a low-pitched wind instrument which was soon joined by a higher pitched flute-like instrument and the traditional Zambillan percussion box.

The murmurs and the musical instruments smoothly blended in a haunting melody to which the congregation began to sway. The effect was infectious, Alice found herself beginning to sway from side to side as Marisa was already doing.

After a few moments, the instruments and percussion faded away much as they had made their appearance, and were replaced by the sound of a male voice that gradually morphed into words. Marisa whispered that the man was speaking in a local Indian dialect and calling for the Great Healer.

Behind a stone altar stood an eight-foot high boulder from behind which an elaborately and colorfully dressed figure emerged. His head was covered by a huge headpiece with several arm-like extensions and numerous protruding eyeballs with red pupils. An immaculate white cloth with dangling multicolored tassels rested on his shoulders; rectangular strips of multicolored cloth reached from his shoulders to his knees like serpents with human faces; loose fitting white pants and matching sandals completed his ceremonial vestments.

From behind each side of the boulder an acolyte wearing a headpiece identical to the one worn by the great Healer but only half as large appeared holding earthen vessels which they placed on the altar in front of the Great Healer. Over the next few minutes the Great Healer made elaborate hand gestures over the two vessels and uttered a serious of ritual incantations, of adulation and entreatments to the gods. At regular intervals, the acolytes lifted the vessels high into the air while the Great Healer extended his arms in front of him with palms facing sky-wards in offertory.

While this was happening, a female voice sounded from behind the rock singing a plaintive melody. Simultaneously, down the center of the seated assemblage in a path which, as if by some previously rehearsed choreography, opened before her, a young woman walked slowly towards the altar. She wore a white pleated blouse, and a floor-length brown skirt. Over her shoulders rested a shawl striped with an entire spectrum of colors. Her feet were bare.

As the young woman neared the altar the two acolytes stepped back and the Great Healer came around to the front of the altar. She stopped a few feet in front of him. Then began a series of questions and answers which Marisa did her best to translate though the language seemed to be a mixture of dialects not all of which were familiar to her. The Great Healer's voice sounded surprisingly strong and clear despite the fact its source was behind the huge headpiece.

GH	What is your name?
YW	Runa Callanuapa
GH	Why are you here before me?
YW	I want to help my sister, she is my twin, but we are one and she is in need of help.
GH	Runa Callanuapa explain yourself before me and the gods of light.
YW	I am afraid for my sister, the Evil One from the center of Earth is trying to take her away from me, from my family, and has sent his spirits to seduce her.
GH	What is your sister's name, tell me her name.
YW	Cuycusa, she is a nun and she is now called Sister de las Mercedes, she lives in the Convent of St. Agnes.

Ted leaned towards Marisa and in the voice of one who had just solved a riddle said, "This priest or whoever he is is supposed to cure the Convent mess, right?." Marisa hand-signaled him to be patient.

GH	You are about to journey to a holy place of enlightenment where the identity of the evil spirit will be revealed to you. Do you understand Runa Callanuapa

As if under a spell the young woman fell to her knees and began humming the melody that had been sung by the female voice from behind the boulder.

A young child dressed in a simple white gown appeared from behind the boulder carrying an ornately detailed golden vessel. Slowly she walked to the Great Healer with a swaying motion that echoed the mood set by the melody. Reaching the Great Healer, she stood at his side facing him with the golden vessel in her tiny hands. The Great Healer turned to face her as the two acolytes, each with a vessel in his hands, descended from the altar and stood on each side of the young woman and poured the liquid contents of their vessels into the golden vessel which the Great Healer then took from the child. The child walked away and disappeared behind the boulder. The acolytes gently raised the kneeling woman to her feel and stepped back behind the Great Healer.

"Looks like he's going to have the young lady drink whatever that is in the cup," whispered Ted to Alice, and then to Marisa, "some Christian churches use a similar ritual, the wine is supposed to represent the blood of Christ I believe."

"Any idea what that liquid is?" asked Alice in cupped hands.

"I suspect it's the juice from the floripondium."

"Flori what," asked a perplexed Ted, "What is that?"

"Quiet, quiet, we are going to get thrown out," warned Alice.

"It produces halucigenic effects," whispered Marisa.

The Great Healer offered the golden vessel to the woman and then said to her, "Runa Callanuapa drink of this and yield to the powers of the gods, for they will make great revelations to you." She took the vessel and drank, then sank to the ground as if weighted down by the liquid. The Great Healer turned and disappeared behind the boulder. The acolytes lifted the now trembling woman by the arms and sat her against the altar where they stood guard over her.

Marisa signaled Ted and Alice that they should leave. Only a few of the assemblage did the same, most remained seated and conversed in low tones.

Once a safe hearing distance away from the scene of the ritual, Ted asked anxiously, "what was that all about Marisa, what happens to that woman, she looks in pretty bad shape."

"What we have just seen is a really ancient ritual. What is supposed to happen is that the nearest person, preferably a relative, to an infected or sick person, by ingesting the juice from the floripondium plant as part of a ritual like the one we saw, is eased away to a place which is hard to translate into English. It's what I guess psychologists would call an altered state of consciousness where she will obtain direct knowledge about the source of evil that has afflicted the affected person. Of course the Great Healer does not speak in these terms, he will say the woman will travel to a place inhabited by the spirit of the gods where the identity of the person or thing in which the evil spirit dwells will be made known to her."

Ted said he didn't understand the part about evil spirit.

Marisa explained that to believers there exists a Supreme Evil One who inhabits the center of the earth, who sends what she supposed would in English be called agent spirits to inhabit the bodies of humans, or of natural objects and through them spread depravity throughout the world. From what they had just witnessed it seems that one of these agent spirits is believed to have entered the body of someone who in turn has caused the woman's sister, who is one of the Convent nuns, to behave as she has.

Ted said this was all pretty primitive stuff. It was hard to believe that in this time in history with all the advances of science that such irrational beliefs in something like a master devil who lives in the center of the earth, then pausing a moment said, "but on the other hand you know the center of the earth is supposed to be extremely hot maybe that's where the idea of Hell came from."

Recalling one of her more interesting anthropology classes, Alice rebutted that these beliefs were more prevalent today than one would assume, and not confined only to places like Africa or the jungles of Brazil. It exists in the good old USA. Just look at the Satanic cults and Devil worshipping Black Masses that every once in a while come up in the news. How about sprinkling holy water over people and things to ward of evil. As a matter of fact, what is this exorcism thing about if not evil spirits.

"But tell me Marisa, what happens to the woman now, where will she be taken."

From what Marisa understood it could take up to two days for the effects of the floripondium to completely wear off which is when the woman will supposedly be able to report on what she had learned. The information will then be given to the Great Healer who decides what is to be done. Until that happens, she will remain where she is in front of the altar, constantly watched over by at least one acolyte for a period of two hours and then will be taken and secluded somewhere.

CHAPTER 11

▼

How many rooftops had he seen from hotel rooms around the world over the past 10 years on his business-promotion trips. Here he was again, this time looking at waves of orange-tiled roofs in Santa Fe, Zambilla. This was his first trip back here since the fish export venture in 1992. He couldn't help feeling wistful over the heady money days of the middle and late 1990s, only to see them spiral downwards over the last three years. But if he had one saving trait of character it was resilience. He was confident this Zambillan project represented a definite watershed of fortunes.

His phone rang, "Meester Crawford this is Sergio Berrios, I am here in the lobby, Señor Niño is with me. Ten minutes later Hector Crawford, Sergio Berrios and Juan Carlos Niño were sitting in the cocktail lounge of the Plaza Hotel. Berrios was the first lieutenant of Mario Santo Lunes, owner of the country's largest soft-drink company. Juan Carlos Niño was the Director of the government's Import/Export Agency, and a school buddy of Berrios.

After a brief exchange of social pleasantries, Crawford handed out newspaper clippings from his briefcase.

"As you can see," he said, "this satanic possession thing is popping up around the world. Look here at this article from a Springfield, Illinois newspaper, *Two Sisters Stricken—Claimed to be Cases of a Satanic Possession*. Sergio, look at your clipping, five cases reported in Ecuador, four in Colombia and 10 in Venezuela. Señor Niño, look at your clipping, 10 cases in Central America. My calculations show that as of yesterday so-called possession cases have been reported in six countries, not including your own where the situation is approaching panic level.

Excuse my language but this thing is spreading and has a lot of people scared shit-less."

Berrios wanted to know whether Crawford believed there were really demons out there. Instead of answering, Crawford suggested they go upstairs to his room where they will have the necessary privacy. And it was not until the three were sitting in Crawford's room that he answered Berrio's question.

"I don't have a clue and what's more I care even less. Let someone else figure it out. If I can make a few bucks, I'm satisfied. Listen, I've lined up supply sources in Rome, Fatima, Lourdes and Assis. Bethlehem may soon join the list. That's what really matters."

Though he knew both men represented linchpins in his project, Crawford felt it necessary to test them with his pet brinkmanship gambit.

"Now if either of you feel that things other than money will govern your attitude towards the project, then let me know right here and now so that I can know whether I go with you on this business or whether I do it with others, who, I assure you, are ready and willing to join me."

Niño's occasional nervous face tic accelerated in number and in force. But Sergio Berrios knew very well that the American was bluffing and that without his boss' collaboration the project would be dead in the water, even more so if there was to be no government cooperation. Though he wasn't pleased by Crawford's threadbare game and what it might presage, Berrios was sure his group would be able to keep this gringo honest, so he went along with the bluff.

"We are here because we want to participate in your new business and that should be a sufficient answer to your question. Now why don't we get down to business Meester Crawford."

"Great, that's what I wanted to hear. Now let's go over the ground again. As I said, our supply sources in Rome, Fatima, Lourdes and Assis are set up and ready to go. As soon as I finish up here, I'm flying to Israel to nail down Jerusalem, which, incidentally, may turn out to be the gem among all of them if you consider that it is the only city where the three major religions of the world—Jewish, Christian and Islamic—have deep roots and shrines, and that all three believe in this thing of devils invading human bodies."

Crawford's plan was to ship water in tankers to Zambilla from those cities, have it bottled by Santo Lunes' company and then distributed throughout Zambilla via the company's existing network. This would greatly reduce the cost compared to having the bottling done in Europe. Juan Carlos Niño was to arrange that under the Zambillan governments' revised import regulations water will not be prohibited as it currently is.

Niño assured Crawford that the new regulations would be published and go into effect the following day. There will be a five percent duty imposed on the imports. Knowing that this tax aspect had not been mentioned earlier and that Crawford would be upset, Niño immediately turned to a subject pleasing to the American.

It was important to bear in mind that under international treaties it was not possible to permit imports of a product from some countries and not from others, consequently, under the new regulations all water imports will be taken off the list of prohibited imports. However, and this Niño emphasized by pronouncing each word slowly and distinctly and with a touch of *braggadocio*, "Water imports will be subject to government issued licenses which means it will be possible to prevent or at least frustrate imports not only from countries different from ours but also from those from our countries which are sent by exporters different from Meester Crawford's suppliers."

Crawford had put together too many ventures not to realize that the government, by requiring import licenses, had placed itself in a position where it could also shut down his business by simply denying licenses so, in effect, the license agreement was a double-edge sword. But this was the best deal he could cut and he had to work with it for this was a pilot-project which if successful would be used in a number of countries. It meant he would have to keep certain government people happy so they would have no incentive to pull the plug on him. Instead of mentioning any of this, he said the business could work with the five percent tax, but there were to be no more taxes or duties or whatever or the deal would be off.

Berrio said his boss wanted a clear, unambiguous contract especially as to his company's production and distribution fees. These would be no less than twenty-five percent of the retail sales price. Crawford pointed out that since a subsidiary of Santo Lunes' company would be supplying the containers, he expected the prices will be reasonable. Berrios said Mr. Santo Lunes was an honest businessman, then he handed Crawford an eight-inch tall glass bottle roughly with the shape of what could be interpreted to be the figure of Jesus.

Shaking his head vigorously, Crawford handed the bottle back to Berrios.

"No, no this will not do, it will only create controversy, no figures or images of Christ please. Use an ordinary shaped bottle and place a label on it with a scene of the place from where the water originates, Fatima, for example, together with the image of the Saint associated with the place. Look, on second thought I'll design the label myself."

Crawford had no desire to be accused of running a fraudulent operation. His ten days and his former partner's two years in a Brazilian jail convinced him of this. His Zambillan collaborators had to be made to understand how important it was that the water not be held out to be holy water like the one used in churches, and that it was not drinking water. It will simply be water that is certified as coming from the ground or other natural sources in those cities of miracles. All containers sent from there will bear a Seal of Authenticity issued by the local government. Crawford intended to imprint a copy of the seal on each retail bottle label.

"We'll leave it to whatever preconceptions, credos, prejudices and superstitions people may have in their heads to draw their own connections between the water and the Convent. All we are going to say is that it is not to be taken internally, period.

"Gentlemen, this brings me to an announcement I've been holding for this moment. This I guaranty you will like, but first a brief background." He went on to point out that in the past and still true in many areas of business, including those in the developed countries, the systems used for marketing products involved a lot of hit and miss. Today, by turning to the traditional sciences for ideas, it is becoming possible to eliminate much of the guesswork. One result of this collaboration is the idea of neuromarketing. He was no expert on the subject but could say in general layman's terms that it involved the study—by the use of M.R.I. machines—of a brain's neuron reactions when the person is shown a product, or when one is described to him. Based on a review of the scan results, it has been possible to pretty accurately predict whether a product could be successfully marketed.

Leaning back in his chair in the proud posture of someone who was about to convey good news, he continued, "Now to the part of interest to you gentlemen. Over the past few days we have been conducting a series of neuro studies on a representative sample of your fellow countrymen. Gentlemen the results are in and it has been found that when references were made to water from our four cities, the M.R.I. showed a spike-up of activity in the *medial prefrontal cortex* region of the brain, where it signals whether or not it is attracted to an object and is excited about it, in this case the water.

The results of the tests were analyzed by expert neuroscientists and it was found that 80 percent of those tested reacted positively to the water. When the test was repeated, this time combined with references to the Convent, the favorable responses rose to an amazing 94.5 percent. What more need he say about the future of the project?

"Gentlemen, the age of neuromarketing of the developed nations of the world has arrived at the shores Zambilla.

✳   ✳   ✳   ✳

Across the country, Paul Schaeffer of Randolf Publishing of New York sat in the vestibule of the Saint Anthony parish offices. This was too important an assignment to be given to an associate, so the president of the company decreed that Schaeffer was the person to travel to Zambilla to speak to Father Manfredo. Schaeffer thought it probably didn't hurt that he was a Catholic.

Before departing for Zambilla, Schaeffer read the few reports available on priests. He found that the Church was niggardly in making this type of information available to public. But from what he did read he concluded this priest had a strong vanity streak in him. Perhaps that was what would make a deal possible.

He looked at the clock on the opposite wall, it read 4 pm, the scheduled time of his appointment. A door opened and Father Manfredo entered the vestibule and smilingly welcomed the visitor. Schaffer was surprised by the priest's handsomeness, though the reports had mentioned this.

Seated in the parish office, Schaeffer commented on the large number of people in the church and others waiting outside to enter. "It's the Convent situation isn't it?" he asked. The priest nodded affirmatively and, with obviously no interest in pursuing the subject any further, asked what he could do for the visitor.

"I represent the Randolf Publishing Company of New York which, under many criteria, is the top publisher in the business. Our reputation is recognized worldwide," said Schaeffer as he handed the priest his personal card. "Of all the books published in the United States, ours are the most often reviewed in the New York Times Book Review."

The priest said he was familiar with its publications and, as a matter of fact, had some in his personal library. He thought the quality of the books over the past year or so had not been up to past standards and presumed this was merely a reflection of the type of manuscripts that were being submitted by writers. "Was it not your company that published the book, "An Outdated Church, As Seen By A Modern Priest."

This curve-ball was not exactly what Schaeffer welcomed as an introduction to his presentation, and its implications could not be left un-refuted. The best he came up with was that RPC had also published a biography of Mother Teresa, and, second, that the whole publishing industry has been affected by the country's recession, yet RPC has managed to fare better than its competitors. Schaeffer immediately realized the latter point was stupidly *non-sequitor*.

Building on the initiative he had taken, the priest asked whether his visitor was Catholic. Yes, he was but not the practicing type, then he realized he shouldn't have added the qualification. Why did he not practice, was it that his work at RPC kept him totally engaged. Did he work on Sundays?

"How can I help you," asked the priest. For a moment Schaeffer wasn't sure whether the reference was to the reason for his visit or for having fallen away from his religion, self-servingly he assumed it was the former.

Schaeffer explained his company's interest in publishing a book on the happenings at the Convent, how the public was hungry for the truth surrounding the events, and how tired people were of the scant, summary-type TV reports and the skewed, sensationalist articles in the press. RPC has already tied up the movie rights to this future book, which indicated how timely the topic was and the confidence in the publisher's book selections.

"Father Manfredo, we believe that you, having been the Convent's priest in attendance, are the best qualified to write the definitive book on this. We are willing to pay the tidy sum of one million dollars as an advance on royalties which we can deposit wherever you choose, for yourself or for anyone you select."

Turning a horizontal pen around and around on his finger tips, the priest lowered his head and fixed his gaze on Schaeffer's personal card lying next to a book by Saint Thomas Aquinas. For a brief second the priest felt a flash of dizziness. Schaeffer shifted his position slightly in preparation for the priest's response, thinking, this guy is sharp, he'll come up with something clever.

After a few anxious moments the expression on the priest's face softened, he lifted the pen and now held it vertically between his fingertips of both hands as a sign that he had arrived at a conclusion. Looking directly into Schaeffer's eyes, the priest thanked RPC for its offer but, as if reciting from a book of rules, said a priest was not permitted to undertake such an endeavor. It did not matter that the Church would be the recipient of the million dollars and royalties. As he pronounced these final words, he stood up, extended his hand and again thanked the visitor, signaling the end of the meeting.

"I'm deeply disappointed but I do understand," said Schaeffer as he pulled papers from his briefcase. You have my card so should you see your way to accepting our offer or should you have any questions or even suggestions, please contact me."

He placed a folder on the priest's desk and said the priest might want to take a look at the contract RPC was hoping to sign with him, and that he should notice they had even filled in his name."

*   *   *   *

"My name is Maribel and I am your guide on this Worldwide Travel Adventure's flight to Chucaya today. Now let me see if I have this right. The languages we have on board today are Spanish, English and French, is that right? Have I left anyone out?" My goodness aren't you all being real easy on me today, only three languages. Can you believe I've had a flight where there were five languages spoken?"

"Do you speak five different languages?" asked a passenger.

"Yes, but with the exception of English, they are all romance languages, so on that flight I was able to easily go from Italian to French, to Spanish and Portuguese.

She said that on the way to Chucaya and the Convent she will be pointing out important landmarks and will briefly describe their history. For those who were interested in delving more deeply into what they will be seeing and hearing, Worldwide had put together a wonderfully illustrated book as well as a stunning coffee-table version. Anyone interested in acquiring a copy should please let her know.

Today they were flying in a Twin-Otter plane which is ideally suited for their purpose. It is comfortably capable of flying at very low speeds meaning everyone will have a good look at the Convent. To make their experience even more exciting, they will be passing over and around the Convent at an altitude of only 1,000 feet, so everyone should be able to get excellent picture opportunities.

"Now if you'll open the packet each of you received at the airport—does everyone have one?—that's fine. In it you will find a great deal of information beginning with a map of Zambilla where, on the top left side and circled in red, you will see the town of Chucaya and in the green square on the northern fringe of the town is where the Convent is located. In your packet you will also find background information on the Convent and on the Order of the nuns who live there. Most of you, I am sure, will find the exposition on exorcism to be informative as well as the summary of the history of Satanism. I remind you again that all of these fascinating subjects are covered in much more detail in the two books I mentioned earlier."

"Miss" said an elderly lady, as she timidly waived her arm, "from what you just said we will be flying very close to the Convent. Can anything happen to us, I mean has anyone on other flights ever gotten, well you know what I mean."

"I can assure you that this plane is absolutely safe. Now if what you have in mind is something other than the mechanical and flying conditions of the plane, perhaps about being personally affected by what has and, we believe, continues to be happening in the Convent, we have taken no position on that. As to whether any passenger on any other of our flights has claimed to have felt something, as far as I know, of the dozens of flights to date only four women have made that claim. We have no information of what happened to them after we returned to Santa Fe. As I said earlier, once we arrive at the Convent Captain Suarez will circle it several times. Now should any of you experience unusual feelings at that time please let me know.

"Someone has asked whether prayers can be said out loud. Since not all of you may share the same religious beliefs, we feel it would be inappropriate to allow that unless, of course, there is unanimous agreement to do so. Obviously, the same applies to group prayers.

"Worldwide Travel has always strived to satisfy as best it can the needs and desires of its customers. In that spirit, we have rosary beads available for anyone who wishes to have them, the cost is two dollars. Also, for those of you who would want to enhance your personal Convent experience we have music available for you. Here you will see an excellent example of another of Worldwide's policies, *Always give our customers as many choices as possible*, after all we do live in a world of consumer choices do we not?

"So now, how many of you have heard and enjoyed the CD that was very popular a few years ago of hymns sung by the Benedictine Monks of Santo Domingo Selar, well we have their latest CD. For those who would prefer to listen to hymns from the Book of Psalms, we have that available also. On Channel Three, you can hear an eerie-type of scary music which some of you may prefer to hear. Incidentally, some of this scary music is actually from the sound track of the 1970s movie "The Exorcist" which I'm sure some of you have seen. These may be heard through our special headphones for a price of $5.00 each. I will be passing through the cabin with both the rosary beads and earphones. You may pay in United States dollars or the equivalent amount in Zambillan currency. We will accept major credit cards.

"Now sit back, browse through some of the material in your packets and relax. I'll be back with you in ten minutes."

Seat 3B	Lady addressing her husband: With the money we're paying for this excursion you would think we wouldn't be charged for those extras.
Husband:	Money, money, money, that's the name of everybody's game.
Seat 5A	Wife whispers to husband: Harry, I can't stand complainers, if you can't afford it stay home, that's my motto.
Harry:	Ignoring the comment: I hope something happens at the Convent, what a waste of time to look at a group of buildings surrounded by a wall. Don't know why I agreed to come on this trip in the first place, it certainly won't compare with the mudslides in Colombia or volcano eruptions in Japan. Those were really worth seeing. We got some great pictures of those.
Wife:	Look at it this way Harry, we'll be the only family in our neighborhood that can say we've been this close to this Convent. Who knows maybe something will happen when we fly over it. Anyway, we'll be the center of attention at the next Shadybrook Home Owner's Association Meeting.
Seat 6B	Lady to companion: I wish those jerks would stop at all that anus talk so I can meditate, I want to be spiritually prepared for whatever happens.
Companion:	"Don't look now but that guy across the aisle has a pair of binoculars in his bag, he just pulled them out for a second. Weren't we told no binoculars were allowed, it had something to do with Worldwide Adventures having to agree to that or these flights would not be allowed, remember?
Lady:	Think we should tell our guide about this?
Companion:	I don't like playing whistle-blower.
Lady:	Let's just stare him down if he tries to use them.
Companion:	Better idea, maybe he'll let us have a look.

*   *   *   *

It's not surprising that Zambilla, especially its northern part, has been a favorite location for cultural anthropologists from around the world with its rich mixture of indigenous traditions and imported religious and cultural belief systems.

Years ago, an event is said to have occurred to which no one was been able to affix a date. The story, which was handed down through generations has it that there was once a shipwreck in a distant place from which Jesus of Nazareth survived. After floating on the ocean for many years, he arrived in the form of a statue in a coffin on the shores of the town of Fumonse in northern Zambilla, where he was brought ashore by fisherman.

The town's people marveled at what they interpreted as a miracle, a messenger from God himself. He became an instant idol. They considered taking him to the town's only church but it was thought to be too risky to transport the more than human-size statue such a long distance, so it was decided to build a church especially for it. At first it was a simple structure but over the years of additions and embellishments the *Church of the Redeemer* was transformed into the impressive religious center that it now is.

A week was set aside to celebrate the adoption of the statue's status as Patron of Fumonse. During each evening of the week there are festive activities of dancing and singing. On the final day, the statue is taken down from its pedestal in the church and in solemn procession is carried through the town as the church bells peal joyfully.

After a while it was noticed that the Lord had a tendency to roam around the town when not observed, oblivious to the anxieties this produced in the parishioners of the Church of the Redeemer. Because of this behavior, a decision was made to shackle his hands in front of him in a crossed position to prevent his spirit from wondering off along new paths. From then on he was known as *Captive Lord.*

All decisions having to do with the Captive Lord were assigned to a guild set up for that purpose, the head of which, Constanza Rue, was sitting in the office of the Bishop of Chucaya directly across from him.

"We too in our town have had at last count three instances of what many are convinced are cases of demonic possession, and the request I am making comes from many of our frightened people and faithful Catholics," explained Ms. Rue as she re-crossed her celebrated long slender legs.

The Bishop was familiar with the story about the Captive Lord. He also knew it had never been formally embraced by the Vatican, as it was considered too redolent of indigenous myth. Would allowing Ms. Rue's guild to take the statue to the Convent be interpreted as an official accreditation of its alleged roots? This troubled the Bishop, so he was thankful for the appearance of a maid with tea, allowing him to avoid an immediate response.

As he watched Constanza Rue raise the teacup to her lips, he thought that if he were ever to break his vows of celibacy just once, he would want it to be with her. This being beyond realization, he wished he could erase the sexual expression from her face by flat out rejecting her request. But it was not that simple, for her father, Juan Alberto Rue, was an important leader and member of the National Congress as well as one of the wealthiest men in northern Zambilla. The significance of the fact he gave generously to all Church drives for funds and was a solid and dependable defender of Church interests was not lost on the Bishop. What's more, the Convent was the Bishop's jurisdiction and allowing the statue to be taken there would be a ringing re-assertion of his authority, something of which he would enjoy reminding Father Giovanni.

"Yes, my dear señora, you have my permission. The date and other details you will work out with my Secretary. Please give my warm regards to your father, and my blessings upon you.

✳   ✳   ✳   ✳

Ted had spent the day at *El Clarín* observing how a newspaper was put together. He was impressed by how well organized the total operation was and impressively synchronized the multiple steps. This he told Luis during their return home later that afternoon. Except for a faint smile of gratitude, Luis seemed mostly not to be listening. Ted saw this and thought Luis looked tired and down-spirited, more so that at any time since Alice and he arrived in Chucaya. He asked if Luis was all right, was it all because of this commotion over the Convent thing.

"I've told you about the Captive Lord thing that's going to happen, it's turning into a circus spectacle. It is demoralizing that those in a position to put a halt to this type of theater end up either intimidated by a few who throw their weight around or are seduced by the prospect of financial gains."

In an attempt to assuage some of Luis' hurt, Ted said that Luis had done his best to frustrate these side shows, hadn't he refused to accept advertising for T-shirts and water, and hadn't he written a strong editorial condemning the tourist flights. As a matter of fact, his strong opposition even resulted in threats by a big-wig bottler to pull all advertising from *El Clarín*.

"Thanks for your words of support but let's face it, what good has it done. As a mater of fact, let me show you how little good has come from my efforts." He told his chauffeur to drive to the Carulla supermarket.

Ted felt good for a change. Not because Luis was despondent for there was no *schadenfreude* involved, but rather because he, Ted Shaw, was not, for a change, on the defensive and needing help, but rather was now himself the consoler to others. He had forgotten his own tribulations and was reaching out to help someone else. Even if this was a transient situation, he was enjoying the salve it provided.

Luis picked up a bottle from the shelf and put on his reading spectacles. "Water, Assisi Italy" below which was the figure of St. Francis with arms extended and birds perched upon them. From his body rays of light shone down and converged on a picture of the town of Assisi. Across the bottom of the label the words "Water from the Holy Town of Assisi, birthplace of San Francisco di Assisi." Above the front label was an impressive seal that read, "Seal of Authenticity of Origin, Town of Assisi" and underneath an illegible signature. In the center of the back label there was a brief exposition of the life of the Saint with abundant references to Assisi.

Good afternoon doctor, how are you," inquired the store manager, "don't tell me you too are interested in the Assisi water!" Luis asked how the sales were going. The water was flying off the shelves, as a matter of fact this first shipment had been almost completely sold. He expected another and larger shipment the next day, including five-gallon containers. People were going crazy over the water. Some customers could not wait to get home and opened bottles in the store or on their way to their cars and sprinkled the contents on themselves. This very morning he saw a woman customer pour some of the water in a spray bottle and then spray the inside of her car.

"You know Señor Agramonte, well he has placed a huge order for the water, and intends to have his two daughters bathe in it."

Luis looked at Ted over the top of his reading glasses. Ted lowered the corners of his mouth.

CHAPTER 12

▼

August 30 was the date fixed to start the exorcism. On the evening of the 29th those who were to participate in the ritual gathered in the Convent chapel; Father Giovanni, Sevilla, Russo and Pierre, medical doctor Blanca Roncha and Sister Dolores' aunt—her father had died and her mother claimed she was too infirm to make the trip from Austria. The evening was devoted to reviewing what was to take place during the exorcism, and how to react to unexpected occurrences. But most of the time was devoted to praying and confessing.

Repeated emphasis was made on the need to confess every sin regardless of when committed and how insignificant or venial it may seem, because the Devil will ferret these out, particularly in the exorcist, and use this information to launch an unrelenting *ad hominem* attack. In order to forge the strongest possible bond among the four priests it was decided that they would confess to each other and not to the Bishop.

Father Giovanni's emaciated and fragile body appeared even more so as he knelt and prayed before a towering seven-foot wooden cross. In between prayers, he thought of the devices and tricks often used by the Devil to frustrate an exorcism. This evening his whole being told him that the next day's exorcism would be his definitive test. If he was able to cast out the Devil—who he was convinced had taken possession of Sister Dolores and had made her the fountainhead—then all the minion demons would abandon their victims. It would be like cutting off the head of a monster causing the other parts of the body to die.

He knew that if the exorcism was to be successful the right conditions had to prevail. As he so many times told his young aspiring exorcist priests, the exorcist must be in a state of absolute purity and piety, free from all manner of sin and of desire for personal aggrandizement. It was through Divine Power and not that of the exorcist that demons are defeated. The exorcist was simply the vessel, the medium through which the Power is exercised, and the medium had to be immaculate.

Father Giovanni eased into a deep meditation to cleanse his mind of all ego desires and urgings and condition it to receive spiritual strength. Before achieving the meditative state, he experienced random thoughts and images that are known to often flash across the mind before it settles into calmness: he saw the desperate face of a childhood friend drowning in a lake, the peacefulness in his grand-mother's face as she lay in her coffin, the first Eucharist bread held before his eyes as he extended his tongue, the dark confessionals and voices of sin embedded in their walls, the sticky wetness of his night bed sheets and fields of bright sunflow-ers. At first, the images were vivid in detail only to gradually fade away and replaced by a state of vacuity, an empty nothingness into which his ego vanished.

*   *   *   *

Impeccable in their newly laundered and ironed habits the two nuns were now within two kilometers of the security checkpoint. Even the car they were in had been washed, its glossy green paint seemed to reflect the spiritual quality of its passengers. Spotting the queue of slow moving vehicles ahead, Alice gave herself a final inspection in her pocket mirror.

"I guess I'm alright," she concluded as she pulled down on the blouse of her habit, yet, she was worried that she hadn't flattened out her breasts enough. As far as she could remember the nuns she had seen were all bosomless.

"You're just fine, relax," said Marisa as they pulled up behind the last vehicle.

"You look really convincing," said Alice, "a picture-perfect nun I would say. Maybe I can ride your coat tail or perhaps I should say your habit tail to get in the Convent."

Their driver, Pablo, got out to see what was happening ahead. Luis had insisted that Marisa not drive herself. The Convent nuns are not supposed to know how to drive cars was the reason he gave. Though this made sense, Marisa was sure it was an afterthought to disguise the real underlying reason, her and Alice's safety. Returning to the car Pablo reported he had never seen anything like what stretched ahead. He was told all of these people were accompanying the Captive Lord. There were all kinds of transportation lined up, cars, trucks, buses, horse and donkey-drawn carts. The truck carrying the statue of the Captive Lord had already passed the check-point and was now on its way to the Convent. Not many vehicles had gotten past security, most were parked off the road.

"Seems like the whole town of Fumonse is here," commented Pablo.

Alice said she would wager that a tortoise could easily beat them to the security point. Pablo asked if he should do what most Chucaya drivers do when faced with this type of frustrating situation, namely, get out of line and form a new lane to the destination. No, no, this would only anger people and draw unwanted attention to them dissented his passengers.

No sooner had Pablo's half-serious suggestion been rejected when two policemen on motorcycles approached, one on each side of the car. Whether out of instinct or dramatization, Marisa made the Sign of the Cross.

"Looks like trouble, we've been discovered," said Alice's unsteady voice. Pablo rolled down both windows, the nuns smiled sweetly.

Before any of them had time to utter a word one of the officers said, "Good morning sisters" and smiled, "are you returning to the Convent?" In a voice so calm and pious that Alice had to restrain herself from glancing at her in wonder, Marisa answered, "Yes, my son."

"Well then you should not be sitting here at the end of this long line, please follow us," smiled the other officer as both proceeded to open the way for their car to advance. At the checkpoint their car was waived through. Alice and Marisa held hands and their faces glowed with a shared smile of relief. Pablo pressed hard on the pedal as the shape of the now-visible Convent expanded in scale.

Back at the checkpoint numerous vehicles had been denied passage and were now parked on the sides of the road while their former occupants either meandered about or sat in the adjacent fields. Some were busy setting up replicas of the Captive Lord on the ground, around which they placed flowers. Noticing that Alice was looking back at this scene, Pablo said those Fumonse people had a reputation of being fiercely protective of their Captive Lord and would probably remain encamped where they were until he returns from the Convent. He was surprised they hadn't put up a major ruckus for not being allowed to accompany him to the Convent.

"Something is happening up ahead," observed Marisa, "look, those vehicles have stopped." Pablo slowed down, several men were adjusting the ropes that held the statue on the truck. Marisa tapped him on the shoulder and said to continue on past the parked vehicles and to hurry to the Convent. Pablo pushed harder on the pedal.

There were no sounds emanating from the Convent as Marisa and Alice got out of their car, and with a sense of urgency walked to the main entrance. Marisa rang the bell. The door opened and the two seminarians standing inside were surprised to see the nuns.

"What are you doing outside?" asked the taller of the two.

"We've been accompanying the Captive Lord. You know of his arrival don't you?"

"Of course we do Sister," answered the shorter one.

"Well, he will be here in a few minutes, so move, move quickly, look there he is," as the truck came into sight, "we have no time to lose, open the gate."

She practically pushed the two confused soon-to-be-men-of-the-cloth out of the way and entered the Convent.

Alice whispered, "Masterful performance, Nicole Kidman couldn't have done it any better, definitely Academy Award caliber, they're probably still scratching their heads over this."

At that same moment and some fifty yards away, Luis was taking his seat in a room above the chapel in which the exorcism was to be conducted, in front of him a monitor had been connected to strategically placed cameras in the chapel. With Luis were the four other observers selected from the Bishop's list, Rob Tennison of the BBC, Hamilton Westly, representative of the Council of Christian Churches of the U.S., Rodrigo Mestre, President of the United Workers Union, the largest labor group in Zambilla, and Carmen Rosa Mendoza, Secretary of the National Government's Department of Cultural Affairs.

Father Sevilla greeted and chatted with each of the invitees and then gave a brief resume of how Father Giovanni had prepared himself for the exorcism. He followed this up with a few housekeeping rules on things such as talking, questions, leaving the room and the prohibited use of cell phones and recorders.

"Fortunately, if this word is proper under the circumstances," said Father Sevilla, "the Demon who has possessed Sister Dolores began manifesting himself about an hour ago which indicates that perhaps Father Giovanni may be able to establish early contact with him."

The door of the room opened and a wizened monk entered and took a seat in a back corner of the room. Father Sevilla pressed a button on the video console and the dark screen became a view of the chapel. Lying in her bed at the foot of a small altar Sister Dolores, the abbess, seemed tranquil enough. Standing next to the bed wearing a purple alb and stole stood Father Giovanni, the exorcist, next to him holding a single-volume Bible containing both the Old and New Testament was Father Russo and behind him the abbess' aunt. Seated in the last row of benches were Father Pierre and Doctor Roncha. The only source of light came from flickering candles.

Father Giovanni made a sweeping Sign of the Cross over the nun and placed his right hand over her head.

"The imposition of hands had been used by Jesus to cure the sick," explained Father Sevilla. The lids of the nun's eyes gently closed. The exorcist sprinkled blessed water over her. "The water is intended to recall the purification the nun had received in her baptism," noted Father Sevilla, "now as you can see, he has begun to recite the names of saints through whom he will ask for God's mercy and intercession."

Luis, who had been sitting forward in his chair, sat back now in preparation to hear the lengthy recitation. He noticed that the elderly religious who had entered earlier was now in a profound state of meditation. Father Sevilla told Luis he was a monk who always accompanied the exorcist, a kind of human talisman.

Hearing men's voices ahead of them and not wanting to be discovered so soon, Alice and Marisa stepped into a dead-end passageway and stood out of sight behind a set of stairs until the voices could no longer be heard. Pointing to a door at the top of the stairs Marisa said those were the abbess' quarters and suggested they go up.

"That's dangerous isn't it," worried an out-of-character Alice.

"She's not there," pointed out Marisa looking at her watch and added, "she's undergoing exorcism. I have the schedule. Anyway the door is probably locked."

Moving with quick steps to avoid being seen by anyone passing by the narrow passageway entrance, the ersatz nuns climbed to the top. Marisa knocked on the door, no answer. She turned the heavy metal door handle and the door clicked open. They stepped inside.

"Hello, anyone here," asked an Alice whose nervousness-measuring gauge was now bumping against the roof of its limitation. In a yet louder voice, "hello, hello there, anyone here." The question went unanswered.

They were standing in a foyer, a few tiptoe steps forward and they entered what appeared to be a waiting room; a sofa, two metal chairs, two side-tables, a dull well-trodden wooden floor and a window facing the Convent courtyard. The walls were blank, but two places suggested that at one time something had hung there, was removed and not replaced. In response to a nudge from her autonomic nervous system, Alice pulled the collar of her habit a little closer.

Standing at the window Marisa signaled for Alice to come. The Captive Lord was being lowered from a truck by four men under the direction of a priest from Fumonse. The statue was placed on a pedestal, a twin of the one on which it rested in its church home. Once it was securely in position, the men, the priest, Constanza Rua and three elderly women formed a circle around the statue and, led by the priest, recited the Lord's Prayer. The priest raised his head, walked up to the statue, genuflected, and then took a key from his pocket. While beseeching the Captive Lord to intercede in defeating the Evil Spirits, he unlocked the manacles from around its wrists and removed the connecting chain. For the first time since he was first constrained, the Captive Lord was now free and, if he was sympathetic to the exhortations of the human circle around him, would "roam the corridors and rooms of the Convent and banish all Evil Spirits from there and cast them back into the eternal fire from where they came."

"My God, look at her," cried out one of the observers, "her feet are swelling horribly, why don't they at least loosen the straps on her ankles?"

"Patience," responded Father Sevilla, "the Demon is reacting to the exorcism, it's demonstrating its power over the sister's body. See how Father Giovanni is tracing the Sign of the Cross over her feet."

Father Giovanni began reciting a selection from the Psalms while at the same time holding the Crucifix over the abbess. Her body reacted with writhing movements so strong it appeared she might bore a hole in the bed. The cheeks of her face puffed out unevenly to the size of lumpy balloons, her eyes opened wide exposing a maelstrom of vileness. A menacing unrecognizable voice sent a chill through the observers.

"Go away decrepit old man, I have conquered, your powers are less than papyrus against my fury you pretender, old useless whoremaster. Here take my blessing."

Father Giovanni felt a coldness on the left side of his mid-section. He tried to rid himself of it by raising and lowering his left shoulder. Instead of relief, he felt the coldness intensify and spread over his entire body which shivered against his robes. After a few moments, the coldness traveled to this arms and then to his hands. His fingers felt like ice and throbbed with pain, his hand trembled. He was losing all sensation of touch. The Crucifix was teetering in his hands.

Now he realized that the battleground chosen by the Demon was in his hands and the objective, the fall of the Crucifix and what it represents.

Frozen beyond tactile sensation, he knew his hands and fingers could no longer be depended upon to keep the Crucifix from falling. The battle could no longer be waged successfully by him at the physical level, it had to be moved into the realm of spiritually inspired will-power.

Each surge of Father Gionani's determination produced a slight return of feeling to his hands, only to be overwhelmed by new waves of ice coldness.

Back and forth waged the conflict of will powers until the exorcist in a desperate effort succeeded in withdrawing from his ego and sense of self as contender and became a pure vessel through which the power of external spiritual forces could be given unimpeded vent.

Fathers Russo and Pierre realized what was happening and fell to their knees in prayer.

Gradually, warmth spread over the exorcist's fingers, hands and arms. Life-affirming sensation followed.

Undeterred, and perhaps even strengthened by the anguish he had just experienced, Father Giovanni extended his torso over the Sister's convulsed body and in a steady voice spoke to the Demon in Latin. *"Exorciso te, immundissime spiritus, omnis incursio adversarii omne phantasma, omnis legio, in nomine Domini nostri Jesus Christi."* (I exorcise thee, most unclean spirit, every onslaught of the adversary, every spectra, every legion, in the name of our Lord Jesus Christ.) The exorcist again sprinkled holy water on the abbess, Father Russo placed the end of the exorcist's stole on her. She responded with a barrage of profanities against the exorcist. Sister Dolores, the abbess of the St. Agnes Convent, was no longer recognizable in the face of the person lying in the bed.

When Marisa entered the bedroom, Alice strolled into what appeared to be an office furnished to be ultra-functional. Though she had no idea what she was looking for, she opened the desk drawers and found only the usual items like pens, clips, erasers, envelopes and a key which she picked up.

"What do you open," she asked herself.

It didn't fit the desk lock and there was no lock on the room door. But it did fit the top drawer of a metal file cabinet. Files and more files, dossiers on the Convent nuns, accounting ledgers, correspondence, all neat and orderly, the work of a meticulous person. She was about to close the bottom drawer when she noticed a notebook at the back underneath blank sheets of paper. It contained dated handwritten entries in what she believed was French, as far as she could tell it was the only item in the cabinet not in Spanish. Across the first inside page in lovely flowing letters the word, "JOURNAL." Alice rushed into the bedroom where Marisa was still looking around and handed her the notebook saying, "Luis told me you know French."

"Yes, I used to teach French at the Alianza Zambilla-Francesa. Let me see, oh yes, it's a diary, it's Sister Dolores'. Maybe you should put it back, we are getting into something really personal, you know what I mean," suggested Marisa, switching the roles of a few minutes earlier.

"Look, we have come this far why stop? Why did we come here in the first place, was it because of idle curiosity or because we were just nosey. I don't think so. There's something mysterious going on out there and the abbess seems to be smack in the middle of it all."

All right, agreed Marisa, but perhaps they should turn it over to the authorities.

What authorities, the police, the Church, who? And how would they explain their possession of it in the first place.

"Well, I suppose you're right. I'll just browse through some of the entries, perhaps there's nothing at all in here related to what's been happening, so we can then just put it back where you found it."

They sat on the entrance sofa, Marisa glanced at the turning pages, stopping to read whenever her attention was caught by a particular word or phrase. Alice sat back, occasionally leaning over to look at the diary and then turning to Marisa with a let-me-in-on-it look.

Father Giovanni placed his hand on the swollen face of the nun and recited more Psalms. Unnoticed by the others in the chapel, the aunt who was standing next to the bed did what she had been instructed not to do, she began caressing her niece's hand when in a spasmodic flash the nun grabbed the hand in a vise-like grip and squeezed hard. The aunt's face wrenched in pain. She fell to her knees and passed out. Father Russo carried her to the back of the chapel where the doctor found that the bones of the hand had been crushed.

Luis leaned towards Father Sevilla and asked whether there was something wrong with the audio, it looked like the poor woman screamed but Luis hadn't heard a sound.

"It will happen that in some exorcisms the room becomes a vacuum in which no sounds can be heard, except for those made by the exorcist and the possessed," explained the priest. "You may recall from your college physics cases that no sound waves can be produced in a vacuum."

In anticipation of more questions from Luis and the other invitees, Father Sevilla placed a finger of silence on his lips and directed everyone's attention back to the monitor.

"Look," whispered one of the invitees, "her face has turned beautiful, and look, her breasts are growing."

The nun tried to spread her legs apart. She moved her pelvis with steamy sensuality. In a seductive voice, she invited the exorcist to take her. He responded by reading the Gospel in a raised voice. The nun grew more lascivious and tucked at her skirt, pleading for him to remove her habit saying her body was beautiful.

"Come to me, come to the pleasures of my virgin flesh."

Holding the Crucifix and the picture of a saint over her body and in the steely tone of authority, Father Giovanni said, "Identify yourself, in the name of the Lord I command you to speak."

The nun's mouth opened to the size of a orange out of which a voice bellowed so low and base that it was felt as a pressure against the exorcist's body.

"We are legion and you a desolate, tormented cretin."

"Where are you in the body of this child of God," insisted the exorcist as he raised the Crucifix even higher. From the mouth of the nun came a squirt of greenish-yellow slime that she propelled against the exorcist and said, "There I am on your stole," and laughed mockingly.

Father Giovanni remained unruffled. Father Russo silently exhorted those in the room to do likewise and to continue praying. As more holy water was sprinkled on the nun, it seemed to be having a calming effect. The exorcist began reciting the Creed, apparently resulting in further relaxation. She opened her eyes and smiled innocently at the exorcist who in response raised the Crucifix over her body and in a stern voice repeated over and over, "*Exorciote in nominee Domini nostri Jesus Cristi*" (I exorcise thee in the name of our Lord Jesus Christ).

Observer Carmen Rosa Mendoza could not understand why the exorcist was saying what he was saying and in such a nasty way. The nun appeared to be peaceful and calm, so why treat her in this way. Father Sevilla lowered the volume on the monitor and explained that the Church's experience measured in centuries has shown that at times a victim will appear to have been liberated from the Demon and has returned to his or her normal state, but it turns out to be no more than a ruse, a clever trick, a deception leading the exorcist to believe he has succeeded. However, on the other hand it may be real and a genuine recovery may have occurred. This can create a problem for the exorcist and places him in a quandary. When faced with this ambiguity, Father Giovanni applies a litmus test he himself conceived to help unveil the truth. After carefully observing which of his words or holy relics seemed to have provoked the most violent reaction from the Demon, he proceeds to repeat the words or exhibit the relic hoping thus to force the Demon to react and reveal himself, if in fact he is still in the body.

"This is what he is doing right now. Let us wait to see what happens."

Growing restless while Marisa was looking through the diary, Alice stepped back into the office. A re-examination of the desk drawers again produced nothing unusual. She sat at the desk thinking there was something wrong in the room. She scanned the room from wall to wall, floor to ceiling. Nothing, she whispered to herself. Then a mental light bulb and a "that's it." There was not a single religious icon, picture or statue anywhere in the room. How could this be, she's the abbess of the Convent.

Puzzled she went back to the file cabinet and opened the bottom drawer where she had found the diary. After removing all of the contents, Alice found a brown envelope that she had not seen before. She was about to open it when she heard the anxious voice of Marisa calling her.

"This is it," exclaimed Marisa. "Listen to this entry made on May 12 of last year. I'll do my best to translate it but I'll have to go from French into Spanish to get to English so be patient with me." She began her slow translation:

> I can no longer entertain doubts (or questions) it is clear that he must be the Devil himself. Why have not my prayers been answered, what have I done to deserve the ugly (or depraved) fate that beckons me. I feel helpless, like a plaything, his tricks (or games) hold me fast. He tempts me with all kinds of perversions. Blessed Lord, help me.

"Wow!" cried out Alice, "who is she talking about, is there anything else in there."

"Hold on, here's an entry dated May 15"

> It has happened, my gravest fears have come true, Sisters Neyi and Beata show signs of being ill. They are behaving in disgraceful and frightening ways. I know them well, they are my children, devoted servants of our Lord. He is casting a spell among my children. I must find a way to put an end to this. He must be persuaded to leave them in peace, even if it means I must sacrifice myself to him. Word of our situation must not reach outside for that will surely open the door to inquiries and interferences with my Convent and all I have worked for over the years.
>
> My Blessed Lord Have Mercy on me.

Entry of May 18th:

> I have known only Spiritual Love, the Love of our Savior. But what is this I feel, it leaves me trembling and drained of all resistance, his eyes are like magnets that draw me to him. I know this is damnable and pray for spiritual help but the Lord does not hear me. Is it that the Lord wishes to punish me? What have I done? Tomorrow he will again come to the Convent to hear confessions and already my children are showing signs of agitation. Our Father who art in heaven, hallowed be thy name…

"Poor woman, she was really in agony. But what did she mean about someone coming to hear confessions, she's talking about a priest isn't she!" exclaimed Alice.

Marisa put the diary down and explained that the Convent had a priest assigned to it, as do all convents, among whose duties is to hear confessions. Father Manfredo is the priest assigned to the Convent. Picking the diary up again she exclaimed, "But wait, listen to this entry."

> Again he came to me in my sleep last night and filled me with the most wonderful delights. I am his, he is my Master.

Later entries were in the same vain, all about nocturnal visits by that person, apparently the priest. Marisa remarked that it was hard to tell whether the abbess was referring to things that happened in her sleep or while she was awake and conscious. Was the *he* she refers to a real person, you know what I mean, one of skin and bones or some spiritual thing?"

Alice thought she might be referring to things that happen in her mind, a kind of hallucinatory state. From what she had read about demonic possession, victims are known to shift from normalcy to altered states.

"Neither of us is knowledgeable enough about these paranormal situations, but who knows, Alice you could be right. By the way what's that brown envelope you're holding?"

"It was in the same drawer where I found the diary, buried at the bottom. Let's see what's in it." She pulled out a letter addressed to Sister Dolores in Spanish and handed it to Marisa.

Things were beginning to fit together like a picture puzzle. This letter was from a woman in Granada, Spain who said she heard that Sister Dolores was seeking information on Father Manfredo. According to the writer of the letter the priest was rumored to have impregnated a parishioner and was transferred to a parish in Madrid. She goes on to say that in Madrid the priest took an interest in his female parishioners that was by no means merely spiritual. Again he was transferred, only now did she learn he was in Zambilla.

"Who sent the letter can you tell?" asked Alice.

"No, she claims that for obvious reasons she must remain anonymous. She says that while writing the letter she was holding rosary beads to assure that she write only words that were true. I get the impression the writer may also be a nun. She warns the abbess to be careful for the priest is said to command powers that are not from the Light of God.

"Anything else in the envelope?"

"Only these two handwritten sheets also in Spanish."

Frowning, Marisa said they appeared to be photocopies of a draft memorandum or report of sorts, a draft because they contained corrections and deletions. The writing is not clear but looks like it is directed to someone like *Brothers in Empathy*, it bears no date, or place and is signed with the initials MDD or MDO. Unless my memory is failing me, Father Manfredo's complete name is Manfred de la Oz.

"What's he saying," queried Alice.

"Give me a few minutes, his handwriting will never win a prize for legibility."

Alice walked over to the window that looked out into the courtyard. There was the Captive Lord accompanied now only by the parish priest. Wonder if the Captive Lord's spirit is roaming through the Convent, if he is, perhaps he can shed some light on what is going on here.

In an effort to assuage the tensions of the last few hours Alice thoughts turned to Ted Shaw. She wondered what he was doing. This last adventure of hers would really test their relationship. She could only speculate on how it would turn out. He had changed, at least in her mind he had, from a charming sophisticated middle-age executive to a worrywart, a weight around her ankle. Her thoughts were interrupted by Marisa saying she had read the papers.

"I still can't tell to whom this is addressed but it amounts to a call for action against the Church hierarchy. It's about priests' vows of celibacy. Wait a second, let me look again to make sure, yes, I'm right, he makes two arguments against the Church's celibacy rule. He says that for a young male, continence, that is, abstinence from sexual acts, is impossible and from this he comes to what sounds to me like the quasi-syllogistic conclusion that goes something like this: for a young man to be practice abstinence is impossible, a promise to do the impossible is not binding, consequently, vows of continence are not binding on priests. The second argument sounds like it came out of a lawyer's mouth. According to him there's a legal maxim recognized in all civilized parts of the world that holds that promises made under duress are not binding."

"Are priests forced by some kind of punishment to swear to sex abstention?" asked Alice, "I didn't know that."

"No, it is not that, what he says is that a priest doesn't make the vow because he favors it or desires to give up his sex life, but only because he is required to accept it in order to be admitted to the holy order of priesthood. This he says is a kind of duress. He ends by warning to whoever this was to be sent, to expect stiff and stubborn resistance to his views, especially from the old-guard ecclesiastics, for reasons that were obvious."

Alice thought for a moment, then said she sympathized with the priest's position, but thought his arguments were shaky at best, and she was about to say that there were better reasons to end this sex-punishment thing when a realization smacked her in the face and she jumped to her feet.

"Oh my God! Marisa, we've solved this whole demon possession problem!"

Alice could not contain her excitement, she felt like doing a pirouette. She had told Luis she felt she wanted to help find a solution, but she had now gone beyond the mere helping stage, she had actually found the answer the *denouement*. In rapid-fire sentences she exclaimed:

"As I understand it, the Church's theory is that these possession cases have a single originating cause. If that cause can be eliminated then all the other possessions will come to an end. They are contending that the Devil possessed the abbess. From there he has caused or directed or whatever all the other possessions. In other words, she is the original cause, the origin, the Big It. Am I right, Marisa?"

"That's my understanding."

"Well then don't you see?"

"No, I don't, help me."

"Everything we've been reading here is telling us they're exorcising the wrong person. The source of everything is not the abbess, it's the priest, this Father Manfredo."

"My God you're right," exclaimed Marisa.

Alice thought her discovery should be shouted to the whole world immediately, but how would she explain the diary, letter and the inchoate memorandum. Marisa said they should hold off on making a decision and instead should look around the Convent to see what else they can uncover. Because all of the nuns were confined to their rooms, she also suggested they end their masquerade and remove their habits before going downstairs.

The phone rang on the abbess' desk. "Let it ring" said Marisa "let's get out of here as fast as we can."

CHAPTER 13

▼

Father Giovanni's litmus test failed to produce any strong reaction from the abbess. To the contrary, she remained calm for well over 30 minutes during which she answered a series of Father Giovanni's questions in her normal voice, and even spoke with wistfulness about places of her youth. Did she want to receive the Holy Eucharist. Yes she did. The exorcist opened the Pyx he had been carrying on a chain around his neck and removed the Eucharist as the nun opened her mouth. He placed the wafer on her extended tongue saying: "The Body of Christ" and recited passages from John 1-17-20.

"Please remove the straps they are hurting me," requested the abbess meekly. Without interrupting his reading, the exorcist gestured to Father Russo to loosen them.

"No, take them off," said the nun in a stronger tone as he loosened the straps around her writs.

Ignoring her request, Father Russo backed away. The nun became restless. Widening her eyes and opening her mouth, she extended her tongue where the Eucharist continued to sit. In a loud grunt she sent it hurling like a missile to Father Giovanni's forehead who reacted by making the Sign of the Cross and reading the 50th Psalm entreating God's help so that the evil of the enemies be turned back on themselves. Father Pierre quietly stepped forward and nodding towards Father Giovanni whispered in Father Russo's ear, "His legs are weakening, you must ready yourself."

In the room above the chapel Father Sevilla asked the observers to notice that Father Russo was pinning something on the abbess, it was the medal of St. Benedict. It had a very special significance and history. Many years ago a Franciscan named Father Dominic Symanski was in the company of a Benedictine priest when Father Dominic, asked about a medal he was wearing. The Benedictine said it was the medal of St. Benedict. Father Dominic told him he had seen the Devil in the form of a blue light circling around the Benedictine and that the medal prevented the Devil from even touching him. For this reason the medal is sometimes used in exorcisms when the exorcist believes the circumstances are right.

No sooner had the medal been placed on the abbess when Father Giovanni collapsed and lay the floor unconscious.

Alice and Marisa had removed their habits and were on their way down the stairs from the abbess' quarters when Constanza Rue and a seminarian entered the passageway. As they saw each other everyone froze in surprise as if someone had pressed a pause button. Constanza was the first to speak and did so in the tone of a scolding teacher who had just caught a student in mischief, "What are you doing here Marisa, what were you doing upstairs!" Struggling to retain her composure, Marisa gave what she figured was the most reasonable explanation, she was looking for the abbess.

"Sister Dolores is not available," said the seminarian, then pointing to Alice, "what is it you have in your hand?"

Alice's first reaction was to put the hand holding the abbess' diary behind her back. Receiving no answer he went up the stairs and took the diary from her. Alice thought how stupid she was. She could have said it was her notebook or something, but instead said they were going to turn it over to the authorities, really they were, and that it contained extremely important information, hoping that telling the truth about the information contained in the diary would some-how justify her having it in her possession. The seminarian showed the diary to Constanza Rue who immediately exclaimed it was a diary written in French, a language she knew very well. As she flipped the pages over Father Manfredo's draft memo fell out. The seminarian picked it up and after reading a part of it crossed himself and exclaimed, "Oh my God," as he handed it to Constanza as if it were contaminated. She read, stopped, looked at the two women on the stairs, then turned the pages of the diary and found the letter from Spain. "Where did you get this!" she demanded.

Now relatively composed Marisa spoke up. "Listen Constanza what my friend Alice has said is the truth, we have no intention of keeping the book or the papers. Our purpose in coming here was to help find the answer to what may be behind all of the Convent scandals. We found the abbess' door open so we let ourselves in. Whatever wrong there was in doing that is more than justified by what we found. This is much bigger than a question of the two of us entering the abbess' apartment."

Turning to Constanza the seminarian said, "Now I remember where I have seen these two women before" they are the nuns who came in here just before you arrived with the statue. They said they came ahead of your group to let us know the statue was about to arrive."

"Believe me they are no nuns, at least this Marisa isn't scoffed Constanza. After warning Marisa she could be in serious trouble with the law, she told the seminarian to arrange to have the two women escorted to the road checkpoint and left there, but to first allow them to call for someone to pick them up. Turning to Marisa she said if she agreed to this then they would not be reported to the authorities, provided they had taken no other item from the apartment.

Marisa's ire was rising at this self-appointed authority who had now gotten the upper hand over her. She never could stomach the haughtiness of a rich daddy's girl. Though the two women knew of each other, there had been few contacts between them. Constanza was adroit in parlaying her father's influence to involve herself in all local or national events of any importance, and in the process managed to have her name and picture before the public more often than any other woman in Zambilla. She was the former National Red Cross president and self-styled art connoisseur—which she based on the fact she had lived and studied in Paris a couple of years. She was never absent from State dinners honoring foreign dignitaries. Every once in a while rumors would circulate that she had presidential ambitions.

Constanza was familiar with Marisa's sculpture work and fearing competition for the country's attention she seldom missed an opportunity to cast barbs in her direction. This reached an apex two years earlier when as the president of a committee appointed to organize a regional Latin American exhibition tour of Zambillan art, she had Marisa'a works excluded. Seeing Marisa standing there on the atepa, caught in a compromising situation, was a sumptuous delight.

While waiting for transportation to the road checkpoint, Marisa and Alice stood outside the main Convent entrance and smarting over being co-opted by Constanza Rue. Two seminarians stood watch on the other side. Overhearing one of them mention that no males and particularly the seminarians were allowed to go anywhere near the nuns' cells, Marisa, remembering that the public bathroom was in the same area as the nun's cells, smiled for the first time since her encounter on the stairway. She told the seminarians she needed to use the bathroom. Begrudgingly, she was given permission but told to hurry back for their transportation would soon arrive. Alice said she also had to go.

"We have to try to speak to the nuns about Father Manfredo, they may throw some light on this," said a renewed Marisa as she and Alice approached the nuns' cells.

Later that evening she described what they saw to Luis and Ted: "As soon as we entered the hall where the cells were located we were met by a cacophony of shouting voices, some uttering words that would make the most depraved derelict blush while they lifted their habits and invited sexual attention, others were grunting like hogs while others prayed, some had contorted their bodies into improbable shapes. It was like peeking into Hell itself.

Earlier, Constanza had told her accompanying seminarian not to worry for she would take the diary and papers retrieved from Alice to the proper authorities. Not having had instructions on what to do in a situation like this and not wanting to stand in anyone's way in such a weighty matter, the seminarian acquiesced. When he reported these events to the priest in charge of the seminarians at the Convent, he was told to find Constanza and to bring back the book and papers. A few minutes later the seminarian reported that Constanza had left the Convent in a hurry and had taken the book and papers with her.

Father Pierre carried the limp figure of the exorcist to the back of the chapel where doctor Roncha examined him and found that the old priest's vital signs were faint. Father Russo continued on with the exorcism from where Father Giovanni had left off. Sister Dolores broke into a jeering laughter that drowned out the voice of the new exorcist. Silently and hardly noticed, three priests entered through the door at the back of the chapel. Two of them carried Father Giovanni out, the third took Father Pierre's place next to the doctor as Father Pierre assumed the role of assistant exorcist.

After two more hours of praying and attempting to engage the demon in conversation, Father Russo decided to suspend the procedure until the following day in order to review and evaluate what had happened during the exorcism. Depending on the status of Father Giovanni, he would prepare the strategy for the next day's session.

Tuesday October 11

3:30 p.m.
Constanza Rue obtained photocopies of Sister Dolores' diary, the letter from Spain and Father Manfredo's memo.

5:00 p.m.
Constanza Rue delivered the diary and draft memo to the Bishop who promised to look into the matter.

6:00 p.m.
Marisa and Alice reported what happened in the Convent to Luis and Ted.

Wednesday October 12

The exorcism of the abbess continued with Father Russo as the exorcist.
Neither Luis nor Constanza Rue were able to get through to the Bishop.

Thursday October 13

(No word from the Bishop on the diary. Constanza suspected he had no intention of making its contents public and might even intend to suppress it. This she will not allow to happen, after all, she deserved a lot of credit for having retrieved the documents. If she were to make a run for the presidency, this would be a boost to her chances.)

Constanza Rue notified the media that at 6 p.m. she would have a major revelation to make regarding the truth behind the Convent tragedy.

The Bishop of Santa Fe immediately called Constanza Rue and asked that she cancel her media appearance, because what he understood she will claim will be based on the wildest of speculation and could give rise to all kinds of mischief.

Constanza Rue went before television cameras and revealed the contents of the photocopied papers she held in her hands, but which she would not release to the media until her lawyers authorized her to do so.

During the process of removing the statue of the Captive Lord from its pedestal it toppled over shattering its right arm into Humpty Dumpy fragments causing the manacles to dangle freely.

＊　　　＊　　　＊　　　＊

Luis turned the television off and went to the bar and pored himself scotch, dropping ice cubes into the glass one at a time like a bombardier aiming at a specific target. "What happens now?" asked Ted as he too approached the bottle of scotch. "What does this lady expect to accomplish with all of this?"

"Personal aggrandizement and nothing more," volunteered Marisa. "This is quintessential, egocentric, ambitious Constanza Rue who has managed to give her grand performance on the big stage."

Ted asked about Father Manfredo. Who was he, did Luis know him?

"He arrived here a couple of years ago from Spain, a youngish 40 and has features most men would envy; very handsome, intelligent, an impressive orator who is able to deliver sermons that mesmerize, and popular as hell around women. That my dear friend is Father Manfredo in a nutshell," explained Luis, "Am I right Marisa?"

"You only left out the fact he is the priest assigned to the Convent, probably the only male allowed to enter the cloister."

"That's really begging for some hanky-panky isn't it? Whoever made this assignment knowing his character was either setting him up or should have his head examined," commented Ted.

"You have been very quiet Alice," observed Luis.

"Luis, I can't shake the thought that this is all *mea culpa*. If I had not kept the diary and papers in my hand for the whole damn world to see we wouldn't have handed this Constanza gal the opportunity of doing what she did tonight."

"Don't blame yourself," soothed Marisa, "what else could you have done."

"Well, I could have hidden them under my clothes."

"Please, now be practical, who could have anticipated running into Constanza."

"I suppose you're right, Luis what are your thoughts on what lies ahead."

"It will depend on how the Church officials react and follow-up on this and how the public perceives it. I plan to return to the Convent tomorrow unless I'm told the exorcism of the abbess will not continue."

"How will you treat this in your paper?" asked Ted.

"Until we have more to go on it will simply be reported as it happened, no editorializing."

"Got an idea," said Alice. "Why don't we have dinner out and try to get an idea of how people are reacting to Constanza's TV revelations."

"Sounds good to me," said Ted.

"Fine," said Marisa.

"I'll make it unanimous, though I've got reporters out there doing exactly that," said Luis.

"We have no comments to make at this time, the subject is under investigation and as soon as we have completed our inquiry you will be informed of our position," is what the diocese's lay spokesman told the inquiring media people, and then, as if running from an imminent danger, re-entered the residency without acknowledging the barrage of questions shouted at his back. Once he closed the door behind him he uttered a sigh of relief, straightened his shoulders and headed for the office of the Secretary.

"Father Llinas, the media people are exploding with questions, Constanza Rue has unleashed a furor out there," were the first words from his mouth as he sat down in the Secretary's office. He had never faced such a tense situation since taking on this job. "We'll have to come up with something for them to report on or they will begin speculating and the results may not be very complimentary. They may even attempt to scale the information barricades."

"Felipe, I appreciate the battlefront pressure you're under, hopefully, we will soon be able to give you something to hand out. At this very minute I'm preparing a memorandum summarizing an initial agreement between us and the Bishop of Santa Fe on a tentative position to be adopted as well as the necessary implementing measures." Rising from his chair the Secretary closed the office door and told the spokesman he had some extremely sensitive material that he felt he should in all fairness reveal to him which would be strictly between the two of them. Under absolutely no circumstances was any of it to be leaked to the media until such time as a decision was made to release some relevant information.

First, and this he emphasized, no efforts will be made to impeach the credibility of Ms. Rue, this was in deference to the political and financial muscle of her father the Senator. There were rumors afloat again that Ms. Rue had presidential ambitions, that she had full support of her father and was gaining increasing favor in the upper echelons of the Liberal Party. In these matters the Church must tread very carefully. So that left them with the abbess herself. In this regard, efforts will be made to show that her diary entries were the product of an unfortunate nun driven by paranoia or other mental abnormalcy. If no medical report can be obtained in support of this, then the official position will be that it was the Devil himself who compelled her to make those entries. As is known, the Devil is the Consummate Liar.

"Where does Father Giovanni fit into this scenario?" asked the spokesman.

"I guess you have not been told, but then how could you for I myself have just found out. Well anyway, it appears that the good father himself is now either afflicted by psychiatric problems or has been possessed. Arrangements are being made for his return to Rome where he will undergo examination. I saw him a few hours ago and he is in bad shape. He has lost all capacity to relate to external reality. Very, very sad."

"How about father Manfredo, what's his status?"

"Nothing has changed, he will continue performing his regular pastoral duties with one exception, he will not be returning to the Convent, at least not for the time being. Felipe, do your best to keep the media at bay for a while longer. I realize it's a Herculean task but do what you can."

"How are we going to handle the problem of the letters referring to the father having been transferred to Chucaya because of his alleged problem with a woman parishioner?"

It's a question of clarifying the records on this, they will be cleaned up.

*   *   *   *

Judging from the parking spaces there were not many diners there as Luis pulled up to the restaurant, perhaps he should try a different one. At that moment his cell phone rang. He handed it to Marisa to answer.

"It's your reporter Rafael Cortaza, sounds urgent." Luis pulled into a parking space and took the phone.

"What! When did it happen? Who were they? All right see you at my house in a half hour."

"Luis you look pale," what happened," asked Alice.

"Every time I think everything possible has happened, and there can't be any more surprises, bang! something else happens. Father Manfredo has been taken from his home by a group of men and has disappeared. Rafael is trying to get more information and will meet me back at the house in an hour. Why don't we go in and order a light dinner and then return home."

Rafael Cortaza felt this whole Convent affair was his baby, after all wasn't he the one who helped break the story way back when the nun stumbled into Chucaya after escaping from the Convent. Now he has the kidnapping of Father Manfredo news scoop. What skyrocketed his excitement was the whole thing had taken an international character.

He was feeling pretty good about life and his career as he waited for the light to change at the corner of Surgentes and Avenida Jimenez. He noticed the 1975 Odsmobile next to car next to him, amazing he thought, how talented the locals were in matters of car mechanics. The Olds looked in good condition. Wait a minute, I know that lady, why of course that's Inga, Luis' maid. What is she doing out. Their eyes met for a moment, she quickly turned away. As the light turned green her car sped off.

He apologized for interrupting Luis' dinner but he just saw his maid Inga in a car with a group of natives. They all seemed tense about something. Yes, he intended to do that, as a matter of fact he was already following her car. He would get back to Luis.

There wasn't much traffic making it easy to keep the 1975 Olds in view, but not so close as to raise suspicions. Traveling south the car entered the city's poorest areas, a place those at the periphery of the economy called home. Rafael once knew these streets very well for he was born here, and after moving away often returned here when he worked with the police department. Seems like a lifetime ago, he thought. Slowly the surrounding scenery took a familiar aspect as the dust of years floated away. There's Paradise Bar, next to the bicycle repair shop. Used to be an old rundown apartment building on that empty lot. That drug store had another name back then, what was it.

The Olds came to a stop at the side of a one-story building on the bank of the Huachanga river. The occupants stepped out and entered the building. Rafael was familiar with the place for it once housed a thriving fish-canning plant. Like many young guys around his neighborhood, he did his time working in the plant, a sort of right of passage to the adult work-a-world.

The canning business went belly-up years ago, a rough blow to the already precarious local employment situation. He saw no signs indicating any business had moved into the building. Rafael called Luis who was now on his way home from the restaurant. After explaining what had happened, he said he was going to try to enter the building somehow, he had a gut feeling something strange was going on.

He turned off the lights of his car and sat there trying to re-construct a sketch of the inside of the building. Surprisingly quickly, he put together a rough mental picture of the various rooms. Hopefully, things had not been moved. He would try to enter on the river side of the building where there used to be several doors through which sardines and anchovies were delivered to the plant.

He saw several more people entering the same door as Inga. No question about it, they were native Indians. Some wore their distinctive dress. Arriving at the riverside of the building he found all except one of the doors had been boarded up. At first, the door resisted his efforts but then gave way, but not without noisy complaint. Stepping inside he found himself in an almost empty room. Light entered from a four-foot space that separated the inner wall from the ceiling. Standing on a crate he peered over the wall and found himself looking at a series of rooms each with the same four-foot wall/ceiling opening. He recalled that fish were transported from processing room to processing room through those four-foot openings by a pulley-track arrangement.

Rafael heard voices coming from the room that was the origin of the light. He opened the door leading to the corridor, at the end of which were swinging doors to the room from where the voices seemed to be coming. His memory was getting stronger. The room beyond the swinging doors was where the former canning took place. It was a large space containing conveyor belts and can sealing presses, the final step in the canning process, and there was the cubicle at the corner ceiling where the engines that powered the electrical equipment and the pulley-track were located. It used to be accessible from stairs in the adjoining room.

Removing his shoes he made his way down the corridor, hoping no one would come through the swinging doors. The room he was looking for now had no door. He stepped inside. There against the wall were the now heavily rusted stairs, at the top of which stood the cubicle. Gingerly he made his way up the stairs praying with each step that it not give way under the pressure of his weight. The cubicle was empty except for a few rotted belts and a couple of empty oil cans. Climbing into it he crawled to the edge and looked below, blinking several times to assure himself that what he was seeing was real—not imagination gone wild. It had been converted into a temple with an altar, large statues of Indian gods in the corners, and multicolored mats on which people were sitting. Standing in front of the altar was the Great Healer himself in full multi-layered dress. Seated in front of him and flanked by his assistants was the priest, Father Manfredo. Rafael spotted Inga who was now wearing a dark red floor-length gown. All eyes were fixed on the Great Healer who was reciting a cant while holding coca leaves between the forefinger and thumb of one hand while with the other hand he formed a protective shield over them.

Rafael recognized the ceremony as one used by the Incas centuries ago, preserved and still used by their present day descendants. His memory was sharper now, as he remembered that the three leaves were of different sizes, the largest represented the male deity Opus, the medium one Pachamama, the female deity, and the smallest represented humanity. They were offerings to the deities in return for certain favors.

The Great Healer ended his cant remaining silent and unmoving, eyes dreamy and focused on the three leaves. The room was so sound free one could hear the silence. Rafael held his breath for fear it might otherwise be heard. Slowly lowering his arms, the Great Healer placed the three leaves on the silver tray. Looking straight in front of him and over the heads of his followers he said, "Runa Callanuapa come forward."

A door to a small room off to the side opened—Rafael recalled the room was the production manager's office during the canning days—and out stepped Runa Callanuapa escorted by two of the Great Healer's acolytes. She wore a floor length while dress, her carefully brushed hair hung loose over her narrow shoulders.

As Rafael was later to learn, from the moment she took the potion at the La Vega ceremony she was held in secret seclusion away from everyone except the two acolytes. The purpose of her isolation was to preserve the pure state of the knowledge she obtained from the gods, free from the risk of contamination that could result from extraneous influences.

Once free from the effects of the potion, she was taken directly to the Great Healer to whom, in a private audience, she described her experiences while among the gods, and in particular, what she had learned regarding the source of the evil that had afflicted her sister and by extension the other possessed victims.

Her entrance into the hall was her first public appearance since the La Vega ceremony. This was to be the time and place where she would confirm what she had revealed in private to the Great Healer. He, in turn, would announce what was to be done to eradicate the evil.

The fact that during the period of her seclusion she received no food, only an occasional sip of a nutritionally rich fruit juice was evident in the paleness of her complexion and the uncertainly of her steps.

"Runa Callanuapa, we, your sisters and brothers, are here in full body and spirit to hear from your lips what the gods have graciously revealed to you," pronounced the Great Healer as she stood next to him with head bowed. She turned and walked toward the seated priest. The Great Healer again raised the three coca leaves high in the air. Standing before the priest Runa Callanuapa raised her head, looked at him, then suddenly her body began to quiver in resistance as if being repelled by some unseen force, she backed away. The Great Healer raised the coca leaves even higher, his arms trembling in the effort as he repeated over and over again, mah-ne-ummm, mah-ne-ummm, mah-ne-ummm. Regaining her composure Runa Callanuapa stepped forward, raised her arm and pointing to the priest said, "In here resides the Evil."

Expressions of surprise came from the audience as people instinctively moved their bodies back away from the priest. The Great Healer lowered his arms and looking at the priest said, "It has been revealed that you are the agent the Evil one, do you confess to this?"

Without lifting his head the priest replied, "I am a humble servant of God."

"You are the servant of no god and we shall drive you out of the body in which you have disguised yourself, retorted the Great Healer, at the same time turning his head to the left where two men holding poles the ends of which wrapped in cloth-like material stood with a nod from the Great Healer, they set the poles aflame. They advanced towards the priest who was now being forcibly held down in his chair.

Suddenly the door to the room burst open and five men armed with rifles rushed in. Seeing the priest one of them cried out, "Look at him, we have caught him red-handed in his devil ritual, take him, he's coming with us." The Great Healer backed away as they brandished their guns as evidence of their right to take the priest away. Brushing the now bewildered audience aside, they took the priest by the arms and pulled him towards the entrance. The Great Healer began uttering a cant while others attempted to persuade the intruders to not take the priest. They were met with the shouted declaration that the men knew how to deal with this menace to humanity and didn't need the support of superstitions and rituals. With those words they were gone.

Stunned silence reigned in the room as people looked at each other in disbelief. The Great Healer and his acolytes exited though a side door. From the center of the now disoriented gathering a strong voice boomed, "Listen, listen to me." It was Isidolo Uscamedta.

Isidoro was well known in the native community for his braggadocio claiming to be a direct descendant of the Huascar Capac, son of the great Inca ruler Huyna Capac. He was an outspoken defender of the rights of the native population. To many of the non-Indian population, he was viewed as a troublemaking agitator, a role that frequently got him jailed. On one point though there was general agreement. He was capable of impressive charismatic feats, an ability made ever more amazing considering the customary passivity of his people.

"No more, no more," he shouted, "again they have profaned the rites of our highest spiritual heritage. For decades they have destroyed our religious shrines and sanctuaries and stolen the sacred elements, they have ravaged our culture and converted us into slavery. They laughed and made humor of our all mighty God Wiraqocha. We must stand tall and demand respect. What has just happened cannot, cannot, and cannot go unanswered."

The assemblage began to stir in agitation. "Are you with me, are you with me!"

"Si, Si, Si" came a burgeoning chorus of angry voices.

Rafael quietly backed away from the edge of the cubicle and careful to not be noticed made his way back to his car. "Luis," he spoke into his cell phone, "there's big and I mean big trouble about to happen," and proceeded to recount the events he had just witnessed. Luis instructed him to try to find out where the priest was taken and to notify the authorities.

*   *   *   *

Luis could not recall a time when Chucaya had been so convulsed with events. As a newsman he couldn't be more pleased by the richness of the flow of news events, particularly since they were not stand-alones but linked occurrences, one spawning another and together creating a tenterhooks atmosphere generating a craving for fresh news. This was all professionally and commercially to be cheered, yet, as a person he was unable to overcome the sensation of a looming tragedy ahead, of the collision of forces that had taken on their own intractable dynamics. As he had lately taken to doing when presented with difficult situations, Luis poured himself a double scotch on the rocks. Marisa was aware of this and was concerned but refused to intervene in any way. She felt he needed to and was capable of working his way through this on his own.

Alice was curious about this Isidoro person. Luis, as if speaking for Marisa, something he seldom did but when he did so it was with her silent consent, explained that Marisa had known Isidoro personally for a number of years. They met when she was teaching ceramics and he political science at the local university. She helped to get him released from jail several times but was unable to get him re-instated at the university after his dismissal for "abetting and fomenting civil unrest," among the students. The authorities considered him a firebrand nuisance.

Luis was interrupted by a phone call from one of his reporters. There was a lot of activity in the Bishop's residence and the reporters were being kept in the dark. Perhaps if Luis came down there and used his influence he could find something out. He agreed to go but was upset by the reporter's inability to ferret out information on his own.

After Luis left, Marisa turned on the television for possible late news. While the three of them sat quietly looking at the screen, each was mulling over his and her own private thoughts.

Ted was sure that if this were the United States the authorities, including local and state police and even the FBI, would immediately spring into action. As far as he could tell not much is being done here in this backwater country. This was probably to be expected in a place where people believe in demons that invade human bodies. As far as he could tell Luis was the only rational person around, but his drinking may be a sign that he is about to give up the battle.

Alice's thoughts were on the Bishop's residence and what could be happening there. Surely they must know about the kidnapping and about what happened at that cannery. Perhaps it was they who arranged to rescue the priest from the natives. How about Marisa and this Isidoro guy. Luis didn't say much about their relationship. For instance, why did she get him released from jail. Why did she remain silent during Luis' explanation? Alice's intuition told her there was more to this.

Isidoro Uscanedta was also in Marisa's thoughts. Luis' explanation of her relationship was accurate as far as it went. What was left out, and this because he was ignorant about it, was that she had slept with Isidoro once, but only once. It was one of those things that just happen to which there is no conscious romantic or sensual build-up, it just happens, a spontaneous getting caught up in a momentary convergence of certain sounds, sights, fragrances, moods, needs. After it was over there were no emotional loose strands. It happened and it was over, an epiphenomenon of sorts. At least this was true on her side. If it meant more to Isidoro she could not tell, because aside from his social politics he was hermetically taciturn and uncommunicative. She felt no need to tell Luis about the affair.

But now Isidoro had again entered her life. What was he contemplating doing? He was hotheaded and might now do something reckless that could end up further disenfranchising the indigenous population economically and politically, just the reverse of his good intentions. These were her people too and she didn't want them hurt.

She had to find out where he was and try to dissuade him from doing something stupid and dangerous. She would make a few telephone calls to people close to him and try to get information. As she was about to pick up the phone, it rang, startling her for a moment. She picked it up.

No, Luis was not at home. Could she give the caller his cell phone number it was urgent that Luis be contacted?

"Is this Rafael Cortaza?"

"Yes it is. Señora Marisa, I didn't recognize your voice."

Within no more than 15 seconds, a second phone rang somewhere in the room. "It's Luis' cell phone," said Ted, I recognize the sound, there it is on the side of the chair cushion, it must have fallen from his pocket."

Marisa answered. It was Rafael Cortaza again. Sorry, he must have dialed the wrong number. No this was Luis' cell phone, he forgot to take it with him. Rafael said he had an urgent message for Luis.

"If you are able to speak to Luis before I do, please tell him the priest has been taken to the Cabalas *Finca.* You know the one I mean where they train race horses. I'm calling from a pay phone, my damn cell phone has died on me so it will be hard to stay in touch. Please get word to Luis. By the way, there is a report that a group of our Indian folks have rampaged through the St. Martin church, I understand it was ugly. It won't be long before these people discover where the priest is. Marisa asked whether the police had been notified but before he could answer his phone clicked off.

Alice and Ted were standing next to Marisa wide-eyed for an explanation as she dialed the central police station. She conveyed Rafael's information to the answering officer. He said the police were already at St. Martin. As to the where-abouts of the priest, he had no information and asked her to repeat the name of the place where he had allegedly been taken. Upon hanging up, the officer took the sheet of paper on which he had written the notes on the priest's whereabouts, crumpled it into a ball and threw it in the waste paper basket.

CHAPTER 14

▼

Turning down Alice's offer to accompany her in her search for Isodoro Uscamedta—Alice would be of greater service by remaining at Luis' house and acting as a communications link between those involved in the search—Marisa sped off towards downtown.

The house turned quiet. Ted prepared two drinks one of which he handed to Alice commenting that they should toast the fact they finally had a quiet moment together even if it was only the eye of the storm. She took the glass mechanically. Noticing that Alice placed her glass on the table without having raised it to her lips, Ted took this as another sign of how she was drifting away from him and moving into a private space. He reached over and touched her hand and gave his thoughts a voice.

It was his letter to Luis inquiring about the blue people that was the genesis of all that followed, devils, demonic possessions, crazed voodoo priests, social hysteria, kidnappings and now imminent mob violence. Had he not sent that letter they would surely have continued enjoying the same fun life they were living in the States. Had he had the sketchiest notion of what awaited him he would never have written the letter.

These utterances snagged Alice's attention. She wondered whether they were meant to be an apology to her or self-chastisement. Hey, hold on, how about Alice Reddy, she thought, and what she would have wanted. If there was a predominant benefit from the events following the letter it was the distillation of his true character. Had the letter not been written, who knows how far their relationship might have evolved before she discovered what she now realized. Not wanting to get evolved in polemics at this time or cause more hurt than already exists in their immediate world, she told Ted there was no need for an apology.

The last drink was the fourth Ted had taken in the last hour or so, something which he was unaccustomed to.

"Think I'll take a rest for a while to prepare myself for what this night might bring, do you mind?" Alice said she would be just fine, did he need anything. A couple of aspirin but he would take them upstairs.

Alone now, Alice walked around the room stopping occasionally to read the titles of the books on the shelves, but mostly trying to sort out her thoughts on recent events when she noticed a set of keys sitting on top of the bookcase with an attached tag reading JEEP. She walked past, stopped, looked back, why not, I'm sure to run into Marisa and Luis there, certainly Rafael. Now let see, the place is called Ca...something *finca*, that's a ranch, that much I know. Caballos, no, no, Cabalas, that's it, Cabalas, Cabalas *finca*. She picked up the keys and Luis' cell phone jotted down a note for Ted and walked out. There at the end of the driveway awaited the jeep.

Anton Cabalas was Argentine by birth and a naturalized Zambillan. He inherited his sizeable fortune from his grandfather who raised him after the accidental death of the boy's parents. He became one of Argentina's star polo players participating in matches throughout Latin America. It was said the accuracy and power in his use of the mallet was *non-pareil* among his peers. During a polo contest in Buenos Aires he met Violeta Suarez, the lovely young daughter of the Zambillan ambassador. Following a whirlwind romance, they were married in Venice, Italy.

As his polo playing days declined his interest shifted to breeding and raising thoroughbred race horses. His ranch located on the outskirts of Chucaya was by far the most modern and quickly earned a top-notch reputation in the Hemisphere.

If there was one disappointment that marred his otherwise agreeable and rewarding life it was his wife Violeta's lack of interest in the ranch's equestrian activities, preferring, as she did, to devote her time to searching out and promoting the country's promising literary talents and in church-related activities. Though she had given birth to two daughters and despite the passage of time, Violeta's beauty remained undiminished as it also took on a certain distinguished classical maturity. This fact was not lost on her husband nor was the fact that her outside activities brought her into frequent contact with members of the other sex. This combination caused Anton Cabalas to become increasingly jealous of his wife. Most of all he was suspicious of Father Manfredo who from the day of his arrival in Chucaya had become the female community's darling. At home Violeta never ceased to tire of mentioning the priest. It was Father this, Father that. To Anton, he was Father Adnauseam.

It was Anton Cabalas who brought together the group of like-minded and like-concerned males who were behind the seizing of the priest from the hands of the Great Healer and his native followers. Having the priest in his power was a true largesse. It was not that he had not tried earlier to rid the city of this clerical threat for he had made a direct but unavailing appeal to the Church authorities to have the priest transferred. Failing to accomplish this, he went after what he knew to be the Church's Achilles' heel, money, by drastically reducing his sizeable weekly contributions and convincing others to do likewise. Carlos Luis Pradilla was of no help, refusing as he did to publish articles exposing the priest. Since Luis had no wife or daughters, Cabalas thought it understandable that he would not see any community danger posed by the priest's character. In the end, it was good old Constanza Rue, a woman no less, who with her TV revelations made possible all that was now happening.

As a result of stopping several times to ask for directions to get to the Cabalas *finca*, Alice now had a pretty clear picture on how to get there. She also discovered that Chucaya was no place for an unescorted woman, especially one with blonde hair, to be driving around, and even less so if the woman had to stop to ask for directions.

She found Marisa's cell phone number and called. Marisa's initial surprise at hearing Alice's voice from Luis' cell phone quickly turned to fear when she learned where Alice was and where she was heading. "Listen Alice, this is going too far, you are going way out on this, you can get hurt badly, this is not a game people are playing. If I can't convince you to return to Luis' house then at least do me a favor and do not enter the Cabalas place, wait for me at the entrance gate. I've found out that Isodoro is leading a group of angry men out there and there's going to be trouble. Promise to wait for me."

When Marisa arrived at the front gate of the ranch, she saw no sign of Alice. Neither was Luis' jeep to be seen among the numerous cars parked outside the red building whose lights flooded the surrounding area. Her first thought was that Alice had lost her way or, worse, that she had had an accident. Marisa had never met a woman like Alice, so American-like was she, at least as far as Marisa's secondhand knowledge American women went; assertive and bold in breaking traditions of feminine silence, of socially designated occupations and of familial roles, not to mention of submission to male dominance. In Ted, Marisa saw what she figured was the repercussion on men of this New Era of female assertiveness, a kind of dazed uncertainly about roles and what was expected of them. If she had a gambling streak in her she would unhesitantly bet that the relationship between these two Americans was not destined to survive. The fissures were apparent and widening.

It was Alice who blew her horn and shook Marisa from her thoughts. No, she had not lost her way nor had she had an accident, she was looking for a gas station.

Marisa said something was going on in the red building. She was familiar with the place having been there several times for equestrian shows. She suggested they go up into the stands from the side entrance to avoid being, if not seen, then being conspicuous, after all, they will probably be considered intruders. From that location they should have a good view of what was happening. Where were the damn police, she wondered, as usual living up to their motto "absent when needed." On their way to the building Marisa gave Alice a capsule background on the ranch and of Anton Cabalas. He sounds like someone Alice said she'd love to meet, did Marisa think it was possible. Don't let this rich ex-polo playing Latino fool you, in the flesh he was at the extreme right of anything you can think of, doctrinaire, egotistical, and obnoxiously arrogant. "You've just made him a more interesting than ever," replied Alice. They climbed the few steps up to the first row of the empty stands and immediately sat down.

On the floor of the circular arena some forty men stood conversing and occasionally turning to look in the direction of an elevated wooden platform in the center.

"My God!" uttered Alice, "there's a man tied to the chair, he's absolutely naked. He doesn't even have any hair, I mean nowhere, not even eyebrows! Is that the priest, you've seen him, is it him?"

Shaking her head in repugnance Marisa said she thought it was but obviously she had never seen him in this condition.

"That guy standing on the platform wearing a riding outfit, is he Anton Cabalas?"

"Him, I am sure of, that's him all right."

"The priest looks like he's out of it doesn't he, maybe drugged. Do you have any idea of what's going on?" Without waiting for an answered Alice continued. "Do you think he is naked because someone was looking for a place where the Devil may have entered his body, I remember you saying that someone once told you that. How dehumanizing."

Ignoring the questions, Marisa said that Anton seemed to be ready to address the group.

Standing on the platform, Anton extended his arms for silence. With the loud strained voice resembling a political figure addressing an assembly of potential votes, he began.

"Here he sits for all of you to see. Look at him, not very handsome is he, stripped of his white-collar disguise, this contaminator of our society, philanderer whose voice utters words of seduction in the ears of our women. I want to congratulate the group of you who found him and brought him here, a job well done. Now it is up to us assembled here as the people's conscience to pass judgment on his guilt so that he will no longer pose a threat to our wives and daughters, and to restore tranquility to our homes.

A chorus of approvals swept the arena. A voice cried out, "Why waste time with a lot of talk, let us do what we have to do right here and now." That's right, echoed another voice.

Anton waved his arms and shook his head in negation. This was advancing faster than he had planned, for he was convinced that the proceeding required at least a semblance of legitimacy, going directly to sentencing would not look good. Once the arena quieted down he shouted, "Let us see if he will confess to his immoral behavior and save us the trouble of proving it.

After translating the part Alice did not understand Marisa in a rare display of anger lambasted the police for not being there. Taking her cell phone from her bag she went down to the street level and dialed the police.

Anton Cabalas faced the debilitated, inert priest and pointing an accusatory finger at him commanded that he admit to his attempts to defile the minds and morals of the women of Chucaya and to acts of debauchery. The priest remained unmoving, head loosely resting on his chest. Anton repeated his command. Again no response. He gestured someone to hold the priest's head up. Again the same command. This time the priest in a slurred voice said he had done no wrong, he pleaded to be let free as all he had done was to carry on the work of God on earth and in fading voice that he was a servant of God.

"Did you hear him," shouted Anton, "did you hear the shame-faced blasphemy and lies. He insists on continuing with his charade."

A man wielding a wooden pole vaulted onto the platform struck several blows across the priest's shins while shouting, "You shall not walk away from your guilt." The priest let out a cry. Another man jumped on to the platform took the pole and dealt crushing blows at the same location. The priest screamed.

As blood sprayed into the air with each blow, Alice felt dizziness coming on, her stomach ached and despite her attempts to control herself she vomited. They're going to torture this guy to death she thought as she hurried down the steps. Marisa was on the phone threatening the police if they didn't get out there fast. Cleaning around her mouth with a tissue in one hand and pointing desperately upstairs with the other, Alice began jumping up and down while Marisa whispered, "wait, wait."

A line of cars pulled up in front of the red building and men poured out, they looked like Indians to Alice. She tugged at Marisa's sleeve and pointed to the arrivals. Marisa turned off her phone and hurried in the direction of the gathered men while telling Alice to wait just where she was and not to move.

As she ran she had a sudden desire to be somewhere else, somewhere safe with Luis. She slackened her pace as if reconsidering her decision to find Isidoro who she knew was among and probably leading these men. When she heard his voice she quickened her pace.

Isidoro was giving instructions and firing up emotions. His stretched eyes spoke of fierceness and determination. Marisa elbowed her way through the men until she found herself facing Isidoro. Caught by surprise the words he was about to utter remained unformed in his throat.

"Isidoro don't do it. I'm afraid of what you are planning, it makes no sense. There are other ways to heal your hurt, let old things go. You are intelligent and creative, use these talents to help our people in a constructive way. I understand how you feel, believe me I do. But if you enter this building you will be setting our people further back. You will resolve nothing except to give vent to a transient emotion."

He felt all eyes were on him. Her words took him back years to the time he fell in love with this woman. Marisa and her relentless admonitions on remonstrating against those who he scornfully called the sons and daughters of the White Assassins, the Europeans invaders. Lovely Marisa, he thought, the half-breed struggling to understand who she really is, one of us or one of them. Marisa and her Luis Carlos Pradilla that weak-kneed, ineffectual arbitrator manqué who had managed to hobble her attempts to return to her natural self. Isidoro was sure he, more than anyone else, knew of the native beauty that lay within this woman. How could he forget the evening they shared when she abandoned her pretences and allowed him to experience the rapturous beauty of her body, mind and spirit, an outpouring of all that was her beautiful race.

"No Marisa," he answered, "time for talk and surrender has passed. You are the one who must decide who you are and embrace that knowledge with your whole heart."

With these words he took Marisa by the arm, gently but firmly moved her aside and gave her arm a slight squeeze, as if of assurance, and started for the red building. His men followed closely behind, they were carrying metal rods.

Alice's report on what was happening upstairs confirmed Marisa's worse fears that the specter of irrational fear had morphed into the monster of brutality. They hurried back upstairs. To avoid the remnants of Alice's vomiting they were forced to go up several rows. But now they were not the only occupants in the stands, there was a scattering of what looked like ranch workers there. On the arena platform the priest's knees and shins were mass of blood as he sat with his head resting back, his unseeing eyes looking up at the ceiling. The flaccid, limp body suggested his head had been pulled back by someone and remained there, too weak to move. Anton Cabalas was kneeling at the edge of the platform talking to some of the men. He's probably discussing their next barbaric act, thought Marisa. Alice asked what happened to her friend Isidoro.

"I wish he would hurry and appear," answered Marisa.

Realizing what she had said and how it contradicted what only a few minutes earlier she had pleaded with him not do to, she felt obliged to rationalize by saying his appearance might create a pause in the torture of the priest, which would give the police the time to arrive.

Her wish was immediately fulfilled as the doors to the three front entrances sprang open and Isidoro's men entered. Anton leaped to his feet and pointed to the doors. In a voice that carried to every corner of the arena he shouted, "The Aborigines have arrived." For the first time in her life Alice began chewing her nails. Anton's men turned to face the doors, some reached into their belts keeping their hands on pistols. Isidoro and his men stepped into the arena.

"We are here to reclaim what is ours. We will do this peacefully or otherwise, you decide what it will be."

Anton was about to respond when the door at the left of the arena opened and the Bishop in his black cassock and red cincture around his waist stepped into the arena together with four assistant priests and Luis Carlos. Without speaking he advanced towards the platform. Anton waived away his men who attempted to form a barricade. Reaching the platform the Bishop climbed the steps, walked over to the priest and stood there looking at him. He made the Sign of the Cross and placed his hands on the priest's head. The priest opened his eyes and gazed at the Bishop in a stupor of incomprehension as if he were viewing an apparition, then as the sense of reality took hold, he moved his lips to the Bishop's hand and kissed it.

This is no longer a Church matter shouted Anton, this is secular not ecclesiastic. This priest has violated the laws of decency, morality and good society for which he must answer.

This is false, another lie from the mouth of the White Oppressors shouted Isidoro, this evil man belongs to us, he has been revealed to us by our gods and will be judged according to our laws. Shouts of support combined with catcalls of rejection.

Luis had remained back near the entrance. Looking around, he saw Marisa and Alice. Surprised, he walked briskly to them.

"What are you two doing here, you could not have picked a more dangerous place to be at."

"We don't have time for explanations, I've called the police and they are on their way here. Try to keep these people talking, give the police a chance to get here."

"Fine, but promise me to stay out of this, don't get involved any further." Luis stood motionless awaiting her response. Marisa nodded affirmatively.

"And you, please be careful," she counseled.

Luis gave a nervous smile and for the first time Alice could recall Marisa blew him a kiss.

Luis turned and headed back into the crowd where Isidoro's followers were edging closer to Anton's men and shouted for attention. "Please listen to me, please! The news of what happens here will travel around the world and the causes or ideas you are championing will be judged on what happens here. Don't you want the world to know and understand the rights you are asserting? If so, then each of you should speak up, I, Luis Carlos Pradilla, editor of *El Clarin* give you my solemn word that I will publish your statements for the whole world to see."

Murmuring from the arena.

"I shall speak first," demanded Anton, "for you are on my property. This priest was sent to our community bearing a reputation of lasciviousness. He was cast out of Spain because of his promiscuity, promiscuity so shameful that he caused a young innocent girl to bear his child. And what has he done here in our community but continue his seductive ways with our women. He with his clever, slick words and deceitful manners of a cultured man of the world.

If we need proof, we have proof. Since his arrival here the number of illegitimate babies born has tripled with the mothers refusing to identify the fathers.

Why, I ask, has the number of women in my parish who have joined the women's auxiliary increased since this priest became the group's spiritual advisor? Whose name is constantly in the lips of our women if not that of this priest? Who is the spiritual advisor of the Convent sisters where there is now moral turmoil and what does the Convent abbess say about him in her diary.

"Should he be turned over to the Church so that he can be sent to another diocese to continue to practice his evil wiles, or perhaps he should be turned over to these primitive natives so they can ask their sun or stone or lake gods for advice and end up covering him with oil and coca leaves? Even better perhaps he should be turned over to the civil authorities so that some clever lawyer can convince a court to slap his hands and release him back into society?

"We say no, no and no! He has committed an offense against the honor of our women, families and society, and we the victims have not only a right but the obligation to act directly and swiftly to remove this tumor from our midst."

With fists raised above their heads, Anton's men shouted their support in chorus. Isidoro's group inched forward, muscles tensed.

"Monsignor please give us the Church's position," urged a nervous Luis.

"Let me begin by reminding all of you that each and everyone of us is a child of God, we are brothers and must settle our differences in that spirit. God through Saint Peter has given the Church the mission of safeguarding his laws and propagating His Word. Serious accusations have been made against Father Manfredo. It is the firm intention of the Church to investigate these. It is said he has advocated and urged other priests to consider their oath of chastity null and void. We have found a copy of a contract to write and publish a book on the events at the Convent that bears his name for which he is to receive one million dollars. These are all in violation of Church rules.

"The Church has been accused of covering up certain alleged immoral behavior by him in Spain by sending him here to Zambilla. It has been publicly reported from an unreliable source that he may be the source of the monstrous demonic possessions that first plagued the Convent and have now spread beyond its walls.

"It is clear my children that the one who is the victim here is the Church itself, its reputation and its future ability to continue to retain the trust and faith of its members is at stake. This matter goes beyond local concerns, it affects the Universal Church and millions upon millions of Catholics. Please let us have Father Manfredo back and I assure you we shall uncover the truth about all the accusations that have been made and will act accordingly and swiftly." The Bishop's accompanying priests made the Sign of the Cross.

The men standing around Isidoro slowly moved away from him forming a semi-circle so that his figure would be unmistakable.

In a tone fuming with anger in stark contract to the mild tone of the Bishop, Isodoro began. "I wish I could speak to you in our own language for what I am about to say is best expressed in its words. But because most if not all of you are ignorant by choice, of that language, I shall speak to you in yours.

"What do you truly know about being victims? We who stand here outnumbered, politically and economically know what it is to be victimized as did our ancestors from the time your ancestors first set their boots upon our shores and planted your crosses on our land. This land is ours and you occupy it as conquerors. You who have stolen our wealth, ravaged our women, adulterated our race, humiliated our men, ridiculed our gods, and not only devastated our temples but had the atrocious audacity to build your churches upon their ruins. And you dare to speak of being victims!

"But now you have gone too far, you have again violated our spiritual culture, for which we are compelled by an elementary sense of self-pride and respect to say no more, no more, no more. The gods have spoken and have identified this evil spirit who sits there. We have our laws and procedures for dealing with this that are centuries old, and will not allow this to be taken from us as has been done with our culture over centuries of conquest. Our ancestors will be pleased by what we do here today even if some of us must die. The Light of our gods shall shine upon us."

"They're talking past each other, they're not listening," said Alice, "something has to give."

Marisa unable to restrain herself any longer, sprang to her feet, "Stop this all of you, have you lost all sense of reason?"

Ignoring her plea, Isidoro raised his hands over his head as if holding an object and shouted, "Look your bible," then made a motion of casting it to the ground. Again he raised his arms to the same position over his head, his men did the same. They all shouted, "Look your Bible," and hurled it to the ground.

"Oh my God," cried Alice as he grabbed Marisa's arm.

There was scuffling at several points where the two groups of men faced each other mere breaths away. Then fighting broke out across the arena floor. Yelling, cursing and cries of hurt echoed off the walls. Luis rushed to the Bishop and with the aid of the priests helped him exit the building.

All of the doors of the arena burst open and police officers surged through and began firing over the heads of the brawling men. The fighting stopped. The officers pushed their way through the crowd to the platform. There on the floor lay the priest. An officer went to him, looked for wounds or blood and found none. He examined him for vital signs.

"This man is dead."

Everyone backed away from the platform leaving the officer standing over the body. A cry came of the stands as Alice held Marisa's head on her soaked pants, blood oozed from a hole in the middle of Marisa's temple. The police rushed everyone out of the arena. Isodoro ran to the foot of the stands where the two women were seated and tried desperately to climb the wall. Luis ran up the back stairs to the stands and rushed to Marisa where he found neither breath nor pulse. He took her in his arms and placed his head on hers as his body heaved with sobs as he whispered, "My love, I have lost you twice." Isidoro, lowered his head, stood motionless for a while, then walked away and out of the arena.

The observation room above the Convent chapel was now empty, except for the elderly priest who was laying lifeless on the floor. In the chapel, the abbess' body shook and bounced up and down pounding the bed violently. She howled so loudly it pained the ears of those in the room, the bloated veins in her neck were on the verge of bursting. Throughout the Convent the nuns were screaming, the air was electrified. Some seminarians, convinced this was all a part of their training, an introduction to Hell itself, fell to their knees in prayer, others ran from the Convent in desperation.

The abbess raised her head, bellowed a furious cry, raised her legs and struck a blow against Father Russo's chest. Then as if with that effort the source of all her energy was now spent, her body deflated and her head fell back on the bed.

Father Russo looked at Father Pierre and nodded for him to remove her straps. He walked to the head of the bed and placed a hand on the abbess' forehead. With the other he made a slow, broad Sign of the Cross. The abbess softly placed her two hands on those of Father Russo.

The ceiling lights were still bright in the now ghostly silence of the deserted arena. Two police officers stood chatting in low tones at one of the entrances.

On the platform in the center of the floor lay the body of the Reverend Father Manfredo de la Oz covered by a horse blanket.

CHAPTER 15

▼

October 10, 2020—Nashua, New Hampshire

The chest had a good number of miles on it though it gave little sign of having been moved from city to city across the States. But again, why should it, it was constructed of solid oak. It had not been opened for years so that neither grandfather Ted Shaw nor mother Cindy recalled what it contained. This morning it sat at the top of the attic stairs at 118 Randolf Street, where it had been placed and left there six months earlier when the family first moved in.

Seven-year-old Audrey called out to her grandfather, could he open the chest, please, please. Ted's arthritic legs took him up the 14 steps to the attic but not without complaining. After trying several keys on the lock he found one that succeeded in producing the desired click. He opened the lid, mustiness greeted him.

"Guess it's been longer than I thought since we've opened this up," observed the grandfather and one time insurance executive. "Let us see what we have in here. Ski boots, gloves, pants, postcards, Christmas cards, an old Europass ticket."

"Grandfather what's in this folder?"

"I don't know so what do you say we open it and find out. My goodness, look at this, your mother's school papers, these are really old. Look at the Thanksgiving sketch, not bad, not bad at all. You see, your mother was quite a talented student."

"Grandfather, look at these sketches, why are all the people blue?"

Ted picked up one of the sketches, looked at it for a long time without speaking. He was taken by surprise and for a moment felt a little dizzy. The first thought that came to mind was the meeting with Alice Reddy at the Claremount Elementary School when he was shown the drawing of the blue people. Then he remembered leaving a note for Alice saying he was returning to the States and that he was convinced their relationship was not meant to continue.

"What is it Grandfather, are you alright?"

"Oh, I'm alright. There's a long story that goes with these blue people."

"Will you tell me it Grandfather."

"Someday sweetheart, someday when you're older and can better understand."

At that moment Audrey's mother called up the stairs to say that Audrey's friend Lizzy had arrived and to please come down.

Ted Shaw placed his daughter's sketches back in their envelope and the envelope back in the chest. He closed the lid.

Returning to his bedroom he went to the closet and removed a cardboard box from the top shelf and reached inside. He pulled out a book.

Seated in a chair near the window he looked at the book's cover and smiled, it read "The Demons of Chucaya" by Theresa Robbins and Rafael Cortaza. He turned the pages stopping occasionally to read a few lines until he reached the book's Epilogue. He moved farther back in his chair, adjusted his reading glasses and read.

Following the death of Father Manfredo and the exorcism of the abbess the Saint Agnes Convent, incidents of possession petered out until within a week no further cases were reported in Zambilla. The protagonists in the events that had occurred went their separate ways, some predictable, others bizarre.

Alice Reddy: The living drama and interplay of raw human passions she had experienced captured her soul and she decided to remain in Zambilla where she did freelance writing. She also clung to the hope of someday finding the blue people and, accompanied by Mr. Charlie's partner Jesus Camargo, actually made an unsuccessful trek into the Sierras to find them.

Luis Carlos Pradilla: Never married, founded and became active in the Institute of Inter-cultural Studies, often had dinner or lunch with Alice Reddy.

Father Giovani: Spent the rest of his life in a monastery in Southern Italy where, abandoned and desolate, he walked around the grounds speaking Latin to people who were not there.

Isidoro Uscamedta: Placed the blame for Marisa's death on the "White Neo-Colonists." With a group of initially 20 university students that quickly grew to over 200, he organized an insurgent guerrilla group that operated out of the rainforest in Western Zambilla.

Constanza Rue: Following her unsuccessful run for the presidency of Zambilla, she moved to Paris where she married a Moroccan businessman.

Ted Shaw: Returned to the States where he resumed his business career. A few years later he married the widow of a former business partner.

Abbess Sister Dolores: Abandoned the life of the cloister but insisted on continuing to wear her religious habit. She returned to Europe to live where she spent the rest of her life in and out of mental institutions.

The Convent: The Church closed the cloister and sold the property to a group of private investors headed by Hector Crawford who then proceeded to buy the surrounding land on which he built the Demonlandia Theme Park. Within two years the park had two hotels, four restaurants, built-to-size replicas of the tannery, La Vega and the Cabalas finca's red building complete with its arena.

Electric cars transported visitors around the complex. In the Convent itself, re-enactments were staged of the key events that took place there, including the exorcisms, the finding of the abbess' diary and Alice and Marisa's stairs-encounter with Constanza Rue and the seminarian. The highlight of all of the shows was the presentation of the arena confrontation.

With the purpose of conveying a genuine, albeit vicarious, feeling of having actually experienced those events, bottles and labels identical to those of the waters from Rome, Lourdes, Fatima and Assisi, but now filled with local spring water, were made available to visitors as souvenirs.

The Captive Lord: The statue was returned to its home church which quickly became a national shrine. It was believed that the demons were finally defeated through the intercedence of the Captive Lord. His shattered left arm was never replaced so that believers would forever be reminded of the sacrifice made for the salvation of their souls.

Father Manfredo: The story of Father Manfredo refused to end with his death, instead it took a bizarre twist. It began when a previously unheard of French company began marketing a new perfume called ***Eternal Scent of Passion*** which, according to what was to be readily inferred from the accompanying publicity, would imbue the user with mysterious psychic-energy powers of the god Eros. Among the fast-living, jet-set-partying crowd it was whispered that the perfume contained at the minimum at least one (undefined) unit of Father Manfredo's ashes.

That fact the French company, which was located in a small town in the renowned Alpes-de-Haute-Provence, openly disavowed any connection with this claim only served to lend it even greater credence. What else would the company be expected to say. After all it was illegal to have had the ashes in the first place. There was strong but ultimately unprovable suspicion that it was the company itself that secretly and deftly floated the ashes rumor among the targeted group. This suspicion grew in strength when it was noticed that each elaborately designed bottle of the perfume, unlike any other on the market, bore a series of numbers. The company's official explanation was that the numbers were used to maintain a record of where and how many bottles were sold, but word among those who followed such matters closely was that the numbers represented coded information regarding the amount of ashes contained in a given bottle.

The internal dynamics of the perfume phenomenon led to the emergence in Zambilla, the United States and Europe of secret cults whose purpose was to preserve for as long as possible what was believed to be the extraordinary beneficent powers of the departed priest. To personally derive the full benefits of these powers certain ritual requirements had to be followed: the perfume bottle had to be kept away from light, preferably in a totally dark place and remain unopened. The way to derive the desired benefits from the perfume was to hold the unopened bottle against the body for a period of about two minutes; when there was specially intense need to be imbued with its powers, the cap could be loosened a minuscule degree. Just enough to allow the sensual essence to waft. In both cases, the presence of a blessed candle was essential, with great care taken to assure that its light not reflect directly upon the perfume.

And so it was believed by some that the transfiguration of the profane and the spiritual that was the life of Father Manfredo de la Oz had now been achieved.

Ted Shaw closed the book and let it rest on his lap as he looked out the window focusing on something beyond the falling leaves. Weary, he rested his head against the back of the chair. As his eyes closed the book slipped from his hands and fell to the carpeted floor. It made no sound.

0-595-34563-8